THE WAY WE THOUGHT IT WOULD BE

KATE GREENWOOD

For N. Always here and always your buddy.

Chapter One

I'VE KNOWN THESE PEOPLE all my life, yet I feel like a stranger in their midst. Maybe it's the setting. When we're all packed like sardines in the gym for a pep rally, I don't feel this way. Maybe it's all the memories I've buried in this sand: my open-air home away from home. To have thirty of my classmates tromping through them feels a little like inviting the football team to rifle through my underwear drawer.

Ever since middle school, when we were first allowed to make the two-block trek on our own, Juneway Beach has been Noah's and mine. This thin strip of sand sandwiched between the Pacific and First Street was our spot to spend a few hours in the afternoon sun before homework and dinner. Seeing it littered with empty bottles and cans, discarded flipflops, and foreign footprints leaves me a curmudgeon on a piece of driftwood.

I peer through the bonfire's green and blue flames and catch Noah's eye. He smiles at me, and I wonder if he's thinking the same thing. All these years haven't had much effect on him; he still has the same square jaw, unruly hair, and forever rosy cheeks. When he smiles at me, it has the same effect it always has, like being dunked in a pool of sunshine.

Madisen sits in the sand between Noah's legs wearing a forest green hoodie I know is Noah's. He leans forward so he can wrap his arms around her like the world's heaviest backpack, and for a moment they get lost in each other's eyes. Madisen giggles, showing off a mouthful of perfectly white, perfectly straight teeth. Her auburn hair is loosely tied in a bun atop her head, and strands keep tumbling down that Noah is quick to twirl around his fingers.

Hannah groans, plopping down next to me.

"What?" I take the chocolate chip ice cream cone she holds out for me. "They're in *lovvveee*." I mean for it to come out sing-songy and lighthearted, but I feel more like an old spinster yelling at kids on my lawn. Thankfully, Hannah doesn't seem to notice, and the lovebirds are in their own little world.

"Everyone is in love," Hannah grumbles. "It's gross."

"Cheers to that." I bump my ice cream cone into hers before taking a lick and try to keep my eyes trained on the fire, the water, or the stars, and not my best friend now planting kisses along on his girlfriend's neck. I guess that's something that's changed about Noah.

We met in kindergarten, but that doesn't really count. Our moms have stories of our toddler playdates and recess mishaps, but I don't remember those days at all. The first memory I have of Noah is of when we were put in the same second grade class and had to stand in line next to each other because of our last names. In any other town, *Katarina Dobek* and *Noah Hamilton* would not be alphabetically paired, but in a town as small as Fort Clemens, there were no E, F, or G last names to split us.

Until Madisen Grace.

Madisen came to Fort Clemens in seventh grade. Her father, a vice president of a Midwest-based company, had fenagled his position to be remote, leaving him free to pick the family up out of the Ohio cornfields and plop them down in the sleepy coastal town of Fort Clemens. Madisen is the only "new kid" I've ever met—everyone else was born here—so there was a sort of magic about her when our teacher introduced her to our class—an otherness.

By lunch that first day, Madisen already had a posse of girls following her around, asking questions about Ohio and wanting to braid her hair. Hannah was one of them. Young Hannah, the smallest in our grade, with big glasses magnifying her eyes, hung on every word Madisen had to say. When she found out that Madisen lived on her street, Hannah was completely hooked.

I was not. It's not that I didn't like Madisen; I was more indifferent to her than anything. The lure of her being a new kid wore off quickly for me, and when she didn't have any interest in swimming, reading, or dinosaurs, I would have written her off as just another kid in my class. But by then Hannah had already declared the three of us inseparable so I could either open my heart to another friend or lose the only one I had (besides Noah).

Madisen isn't exactly my kind of person. Don't get me wrong, over the years we've actually grown to be close friends, but whereas Hannah and I tend to enjoy being wallflowers, Madisen, well…

"Madisen! Hey, Madisen!" Tyler, a senior like us, shouts from a little way down the beach where a volleyball game has broken out. Tyler has been the heartthrob of many a Franklin High School girl, due largely to his perfectly tan skin and his father's perfectly immense bank account. He's on the football team with Noah, but that doesn't stop him from giving Madisen the smile that is rumored to have gotten him sixteen dates in a single week. (I'm skeptical, but I concede he does have nice cheekbones.) When Madisen gives him a finger wiggle of a wave over her shoulder, he presses on. "Come play. We could use a good player like you. Come be our spiker."

I've had gym with Madisen before, and she is no athlete. There are some girls that gossip in the shadows of the bleachers during gym, and there are others that actually play the game. Madisen is definitely more of the bleachers type. She once brought her phone to gym so she could text after faking PMS to get out of soccer. The game right now is all boys and I have no doubt they've invited her to play front row so that the other five players can get a view of her ass in cutoff shorts.

Madisen isn't stupid; she knows this too. "Not a chance, Ty!" She rolls her eyes at Hannah and me but gives Tyler another flirty wave.

The other guys are laughing at Tyler's expense, and he takes another stab at it. "Oh, come on, *Mads*," he says, using the nickname reserved for Noah (and her previous lovers). "Get your butt over here."

"Sorry, Ty. You're just going to have to get your stares in like everyone else— in the hallway." She smiles smugly as the boys down the beach erupt in laughter, Tyler included.

Noah's cheeks burn with more color than usual, but there's also a glimmer of pride in his eyes as he pulls Madisen back, closer to his chest. It makes my heart sink into my stomach. I hate that he's proud to have the hot girlfriend everyone wants. I hate that he cares what all those guys think.

The Noah I knew in second grade was a shy dork who got every word right on our spelling tests but would go pale as a ghost when it was his turn to read aloud in class. Back then he played baseball, and he was good enough to make some boy friends at recess, but he never hesitated to drop them and their game to come play with me. We'd play Hot

Lava Monster or pretend some rocks we'd dug up in the grass were dinosaur eggs, and Noah never minded that while he was playing with me, his baseball friends were getting cooler and cooler. By the time we realized what *cool kids* were, we were determinedly not them.

It was fine for me because by then I was already a swimmer and existed outside of the norm. I didn't go to sleepovers on the weekends; I had all-day swim meets in towns that took hours to drive to. But it was worse for Noah.

By fifth grade, Noah was what his mom called *big-boned*. He didn't eat unhealthily, and he was always out and about, but nevertheless, Noah was bigger than all the other kids in our grade. He was teased so much that he quit baseball. I remember once he cried to me during recess because he thought Hannah and I were going to stop being his friends too.

The next day, on the advice of my Grandma, I wrote a letter to Anthony Schwartz, the head of all things bullying in our class, telling him to leave Noah alone. The "or else" I added at the bottom got me in trouble with our teacher.

In sixth grade, as we entered a new school, Noah had a *new school, new me* attitude and started going to the gym with his dad. He signed up for park district football, and by seventh grade, he was no longer big-boned. In fact, Noah had shaped up into one of the best athletes in our grade. He was playing football with kids a year older than us, and he was picked first for everything in gym. But despite his new notoriety, Noah was still my shy best friend. He kept quiet in class, and he always seemed to be checking over his shoulder when someone laughed in the hallway to make sure they weren't laughing at him.

That's when Madisen arrived. Even though Noah and Madisen only started dating last Christmas, I knew from that first day that he liked her and that Madisen would always be his goal. With Madisen on his arm, no one would ever dare laugh at him again.

"I think he's going to ask her to marry him."

"*What?*" My heart shoots up out of my stomach and into my throat. Noah...propose to Madisen? We're eighteen!

Hannah quirks her eyebrow at me. "Tim. I think Tim is going to ask my sister to marry him."

"Oh." The sweat that had formed on the back of my neck turns cool as the panic simmers down. "Well," I clear my throat, hoping Hannah didn't notice I wasn't paying attention to her, "that's good, isn't it?"

"I mean, I guess. She's happy."

"Try to be a little more enthusiastic," I tease.

Hannah groans and covers her face with her free hand, her ice cream rapidly melting in the other. "I know, I know. I'm happy for Dina. Really, I am. It's just..."

"Change."

"Yeah," she sighs. "Change."

Given that Hannah has been wearing the same exact eyeglass frames since second grade, it's no secret to anyone that change is her Achilles' heel. Even now, as we're about to enter senior year, Hannah is wearing the same black butterfly sandals she's worn every summer I've known her, just a different size. Adding another member to the family— changing traditions and holidays to fit new schedules—is a lot for anyone, but for Hannah it's doubly stressful.

"It'll be all right," I reassure.

She peeks over her hand to give me the same look she gives me whenever I say that—her *I know, but just let me wallow* look.

"You know, it could be good, actually. Things were bound to be different anyway. You're going away to college next year, so maybe this is all really good timing." As I say it aloud, I wonder if that's exactly what Hannah's sister, Dina, is thinking. I would not put it past her to plan her own engagement to be at a time most convenient for her family.

"I wish I wasn't," Hannah grumbles, still in a slump. "I wish Fort Clemens had a university or that there was one anywhere within driving distance."

I bite my bottom lip at about the same time Hannah realizes what she's said. She sits upright again and her big, puppy dog eyes say *sorry* a thousand ways that words just can't. I shake my head so that she knows I'm not upset and that I also don't want to talk about it.

Fort Clemens *does* have a university within driving distance. Or, I should say, a post-secondary school option. Roy Everett Junior College is just a town over and boasts absolutely nothing. For most of Franklin High School, it isn't even considered when searching for a college or university. The only people I've ever known to go there were students looking to be hairdressers or car mechanics and my Grandma when we unsuccessfully tried to get her to learn English. For anyone looking to do something outside of the trades, REJC has classes that cover general education and not much else. It wasn't my first choice, or my second, or even my choice at all. For me, it's REJC or nothing. Hannah's dad is a doctor, my mom is a nurse. Although they work at the same hospital, Hannah's family has the money to send her to University of California, Berkeley while mine, well...

Unfortunately, the lovebirds across the bonfire heard, and the conversation can't just dissipate.

"Are you kidding?" Madisen exclaims. "I am *dying* to get away. If housing weren't so expensive in New York, I would be going all the way to Pratt."

The corners of Noah's lips drop. They're both going to University of California, Los Angeles next year, Madisen for art and Noah on a football scholarship. I guess the New York plan is news to Noah too.

"You wouldn't miss your siblings? Your parents?"

Noah? I mentally add.

She shakes her head. "God, no! My dorm room is going to be my oasis. Just think of it, 180 square feet that are all mine! A mini fridge with only my food, a microwave only I make dirty, no one stealing my clothes—"

"What about your roommate?" Noah points out.

Madisen waves him off. "In my fantasy she's always at the library or at her boyfriend's dorm."

A pink hue creeps up Noah's neck, all the way to his ears. "Well, you can always escape to my dorm."

"Mm-hmm."

For the briefest of moments, I imagine what it would be like in Noah's dorm. Undoubtedly there would be piles of clothes on the floor and *Beatles* memorabilia on the walls. Would he bring the fleece tie blanket I made him back in elementary school? The one I know sits on the end of his bed every night, even in summer. Would *I* be invited to escape to his dorm if I were there?

"My parents are going to miss me," Hannah says somberly. "They're already planning all these things they want to do with me before we leave. We're taking a trip every break. Even just the long weekends."

Madisen perks up, her precarious bun hitting Noah in the nose. "Hawaii?"

Hannah nods. Her parents *love* Hawaii. They've been all over the world, but every year there's a Hawaii trip.

"Ugh! I'm so jealous! I would love to go to Hawaii! Why didn't we all apply to the University of Hawaii? That's a thing, right?"

It is, but I don't say so, hoping that by staying quiet I will become one with the sand and the inevitable question won't be turned on me: *Where are you going, Kat?*

Maybe Noah feels my anxiety because he answers my silent prayer by asking instead, "Are you guys ready for school?"

"Shh! You're not supposed to talk about it!"

"Sorry, hon." He twirls an escaped strand of her hair around his finger. "Ready for practice, Kat?"

"Did it ever end?"

"Coach had us running suicides this morning."

"Try a six a.m. two thousand."

"Can you understand them?" Hannah asks Madisen.

"I usually ignore them." In fact, Madisen is already scrolling on her phone. She holds the phone out and up like she's going to take a picture. "Babe?" she calls Noah's attention. When he looks down at her, she wraps her arm around the back of his neck and pulls him down for a kiss.

"Gross," Hannah mutters. I keep my eyes averted, swallowing the lump in the back of my throat. I should just go home; this isn't the end of summer bonfire I thought it would be.

When they part, Madisen is back on her phone, posting whatever picture or video she'd taken. Noah is blushing when he looks over at me, doing that thing where he scratches the back of his head when he feels awkward. I try to keep my face neutral.

A volleyball abruptly crash-lands in the sand, just missing Hannah's head. Tyler and his group whistle and howl, and Hannah shrinks like a turtle into her shell. I stand to serve the ball back, but Madisen beats me to it. The ball veers so far right that it's swept up into the tide and claimed by the ocean.

"Hey!"

"Serves you right!" Madisen shouts. "Hannah, are you okay?"

"I'm fine. It missed me."

"*Boys.*"

"Hey!"

She sticks her tongue out at Noah, who promptly pulls her into a bear hug, and the two of them are all giggles and heart eyes. It's my cue to leave.

"Thanks for the ice cream," I say to Hannah, brushing the sand off my shorts as I stand.

Madisen breaks away from Noah. "You're leaving?"

"Yeah. We've got our first practice tomorrow, and I'm a little out of shape. I should get a good night's sleep."

That's a lie—the being out of shape bit. As I have every summer since I turned sixteen, I spent the hottest months of the year working at my teammate Rachel's parents' boat rental. Rachel's parents hire every Franklin High swimmer that wants a job, and the group of us spend the summer jockeying boats and jet skis, getting tan, and racing each other in the open water when business is slow. There's nothing quite as challenging as getting battered by the waves as you're pulling through the water. If anything, after summer I feel like I'm in the best shape of the season. But I can't take being in Noah and Madisen's presence anymore.

"Well, hang on one second." Madisen hands her phone to Noah. "We've got to get a picture of the three of us. Come here, on this side so we can get the ocean in the background. Hannah, you come over here."

Noah doesn't have to be asked to take the picture; he's been taking pictures of the three of us for years now.

"How's the light, babe? Are our faces all shadows?"

He shakes his head. "No, you're good."

"Kat, put your bag down."

Begrudgingly, I do. I'm not in much of a picture mood, but I sidle up next to Hannah with Madisen on the other end—our designated spots. I smile, but it feels weird, like I'm putting too much effort into pulling the corners of my lips up, trying too hard to show my teeth, faking being happy.

"Okay, I got it."

I drop my arm from around Hannah's shoulders and scoop up my backpack. Madisen races over to Noah to approve the picture, and I hope we all look fine so we don't need to take another. Madisen takes pictures like it's her job, and she expects everyone else to as well. If we're off-center, if someone is leaning just a little too far forward, if the sun is momentarily blocked by a cloud, we'll take the picture again and again until it's perfect. Normally, I don't mind because we'll all post the picture to our respective Instagram accounts and a Madisen picture always garners extra likes and comments. But right now, I just want to go home.

"Perfect! I'll send it to you guys. Thanks, babe." She kisses Noah on the cheek. "Kat, I'll see you in calculus!"

"Can't wait."

"See you at lunch," Hannah says.

"Save me a seat."

Then it's Noah. He smiles, and my stomach erupts in butterflies that quickly turn to stone. He smells like sandalwood and Tide—I know even though we haven't hugged since last Christmas. "See you."

"Yeah, see you."

It's a steep climb from the beach back to the road, with craggy rocks and weeds that could break an ankle, but there's a well-worn path a little way down, closer to the boardwalk and the twinkling lights of the beachfront restaurants. I walk close to the rocks and try not to catch the eye of anyone still enjoying the bonfire. There's a group of swimmers packed around a second fire; I pick them out as swimmers right away because they've hogged two bags of marshmallows for themselves and are making s'mores like a small factory. A part of me wants to join them, or at least get a s'more, but I know the conversation will be all about college next year and who will be swimming for which university. REJC doesn't have a swim team, or a pool.

The main part of town, the old part, is down this way. There are two streets that make up the "downtown" and then rows of one-story houses built up around them. Noah and I live in this part of Fort Clemens. My family had to convert our dining room into a bedroom for my Grandma, and Noah shares his dresser with his brother because there isn't room for two in their bedroom.

Further down the coast is an invisible dividing line where the new part of Fort Clemens begins. Mom says that land used to be all marshes, but in the '90s, when Fort Clemens was discovered by people with money, they started building two- and three-story brick estates with sprawling front yards and private piers. Madisen and Hannah live there. Their houses are tucked further in, away from the water, but are no less impressive. I used to be extremely jealous of Hannah's backyard, where there was room for a swing set and an inground pool.

From where I'm walking up the path to the street, I can hear glasses clinking and the hum of voices coming from the restaurants. There are a few tables out in the sand where couples and families with young kids are enjoying a late dinner under the stars. Those tables are my favorite. Although most other locals consider these restaurants to be touristy—and they are, with their seashell motifs and souvenir T-shirts for sale—I love them. I love that there are no barriers between me and the ocean. I love the soft acoustic music they play and the Friday game nights they host. I love that we can all be strangers there and yet feel like a family.

There are no streetlights in Fort Clemens. Some houses have lanterns in their front yards that cast a yellow glow a few feet around, and that's enough to see where I'm going. There are also no sidewalks in this part of Fort Clemens, but I like it that way. The front yards are bigger here, the houses further from the street, and centuries-old oak trees create a canopy overhead. At night it feels like walking through a sleepy fairytale town, like there could be a little magic rustling in the leaves or an adventure waiting to be found somewhere across the water.

I walk in the grass of people's yards as Mom taught me. Even though there are no cars and walking in the street is significantly less of a trip hazard, I stick to the yards so Mom doesn't have a heart attack. God forbid I ever did walk in the street and get hit by a car, if it didn't kill me, she would.

I walk by memory, unconsciously following landmarks I made up as a kid: the house that looks like a face, the climbing tree Violet Mack fell out of in second grade, the house with a hundred dogs (really only three). Some houses are dark, but most have lights on, and I can faintly hear people moving about inside. I'm hit with the same feeling of being an outsider as I was on the beach. Maybe it's because I paid too much attention to Noah and Madisen being a couple, or maybe it's because this walk, paired with this feeling, is all too familiar.

Four years ago, right before the start of freshman year, on an equally cloudless night at Juneway Beach, I told Noah Hamilton I loved him.

Chapter Two

THE FIRST MORNING OF my senior year begins the way every other first day has, with a bright pink Post-it note stuck to the bathroom mirror.

Good morning, honey! I hope you have a wonderful first day! Senior year! Woo-hoo!

Mom drew a lopsided heart and half a dozen *x*'s and *o*'s at the bottom. I grab a fresh Post-it from the stack on the counter (a little wavy from all the shower steam) and jot Mom a quick note back: *Love you. Have a great day!*

I tiptoe out of the bathroom after washing up, careful to make sure Mom's bedroom door is closed on my way to the kitchen. The coffee pot isn't loud, and I'm a pro at opening cabinets and the refrigerator soundlessly, but I'm always afraid I'll be the one to wake Mom after a night shift.

Grandma is already awake and sitting in the living room on our once pristine, now lumpy with butt grooves, couch. She's made a cup of tea and is reading a book I've seen her poring over for the last few weeks. I don't know where or when she got it, but since she did, she hasn't pulled her nose out of it. Grandma is half blind even with glasses, so her nose is quite literally in her book.

"Good morning, Grandma," I whisper as I pass. She can't hear me when I whisper, but it doesn't feel right not to say it.

There are chicken breasts defrosting on the counter for dinner. I know they're supposed to be defrosted in the fridge—Mom always tells Grandma this—but this is the way Grandma has been doing it for decades, and if I put them in the fridge, they're just going to end up back on the counter. I do move them out of the way of the coffee machine though so I can get a cup brewing. As I eat breakfast, I also make a sack lunch for school. Sometimes Grandma will bake *kolaczki* as a treat I can take with me, but with that book preoccupying her, it looks like I'm out of luck today.

"Bye, Grandma," I again whisper, knowing she can't hear me. I let myself out as quietly as I can and start the trek to school. It's not a long walk (only a few blocks), but with both my backpack and my swim bag over my shoulders, it feels like climbing Mount Everest. Since there's no morning practice on the first day of school, I wonder if I can flag down Madisen and hitch a ride with her and Noah. Although I'm still feeling a little weird from last night, I'd take the third-wheeling over lugging two bags and walking.

Unfortunately, I never see them. After I manage to cram both bags into the pencil case Fort Clemens High calls a locker, I realize why.

Before class starts, Hannah, Madisen, and I hang out in front of Madisen's locker. Sometimes Noah is there, and usually I get there only a few minutes before class starts because of morning practice. But today I'm twenty minutes early, and Madisen has already beaten me. She's wearing rolled overalls over a white T-shirt with her hair in perfectly messy space buns. She's standing, not sitting as per usual, and seems to be pacing. At first, I think something is wrong, but when Madisen sees me, her whole face lights up and she nearly tackles me to the floor. "Guess *what*!"

A crazy part of my brain panics, thinking, *Did Noah propose?* But that thought is quickly squashed by logic and reason. "What?"

"Look at this!"

As she pulls out her phone, I subtly redo my own bun, trying to give it more volume like hers. Madisen pulls up her Instagram page and shows me her latest Story. It's a short video of her doing a dance on the beach, perfectly timed and choreographed to a radio hit I can't remember the name of but instinctively know all the words to. But that's not what has her so excited. It's the number of views.

"Oh, my gosh! Is this real?"

"Yep! And quick, open your Instagram!" I do as she says, still not believing that many people saw Madisen's Story. "Okay, go to the Explore page. Do you see it? Do you see it?"

"See what?"

Then I see it. Madisen's Story is at the top of the Explore page, which means it is among the most popular content on Instagram right now across the entire world. "Whoa."

"I *know*! I gained ten thousand followers *overnight*!"

"Oh, wow…"

These don't seem like real numbers to me. It's like hearing about our country's trillion-dollar deficit—what even is a trillion dollars? What are ten thousand *additional* followers to someone like me who is barely breaking two hundred?

I watch the video again, and I can feel my eyes turning green. Madisen is a good dancer (she's been dancing since preschool), but is that really why her Story is so popular? Or is it her perfect auburn waves? Her ocean blue eyes? Her born-with-it natural beauty?

I shake my head. Madisen is one of my best friends. I should be happy for her. "That's awesome, Madisen," I say, and I really mean it.

"Thanks! I've already had a couple of sponsors reach out to me."

"Sponsors?"

"Yeah, for like eco-friendly water bottles, or yoga pants, or this protein shake powder stuff."

"I don't get it."

"You know, like the ads you see on Instagram?"

"Yeah."

"So, like, same thing, but I just take a picture using whatever product they send me, and they pay me."

I bite my lip. That seems awfully fishy to me. "Can they do that? I mean…is it safe? We're still in high school, and you know, what if they—"

Madisen waves me off. "Oh, yeah, it's fine. I'm eighteen, so it's all good."

I can't imagine what my mom would say if I told her I was making ads on Instagram. She doesn't even like the fact that I have an account. But I can tell Madisen is dying to share her excitement with someone, and I don't want to be the one to rain on her parade. "Well… I guess that's pretty cool. Are you going to do it?"

"Oh, yeah! I mean, not all of them because I don't want all of that junk. But, like, these—" Madisen stretches her leg out so I can see she's wearing sneakers with a signature white penguin logo on the heel. "Penguin Apparel said they'd send me their new pair."

I feel not unlike the family dog staring up at the Thanksgiving table, knowing I'm never going to get a bite. I've wanted Penguin Apparel sneakers for over a year. Truthfully, they're no different than the white sneakers I get at Payless except for the logo on the heel, but that logo makes all the difference.

"Wow," I find myself saying.

"Wow, what?" Hannah asks. She drops her backpack on the floor, and the three of us sit. As Madisen shares the news with Hannah, my eyes roam over their outfits and then bleakly over my own. Although Madisen's clothes look like anything I could find at Target, I know they're not. Those overalls and that shirt fit her perfectly because the stores she shops at charge more money to make better quality clothes. The same is true for Hannah. Although she's just wearing a sundress, I know it's from a store I've never shopped in because it isn't too long and the chest isn't too loose. Those kinds of stores have half sizes, talls, petites, and all kinds of other variations so their customers don't have to squeeze into whatever box whatever designer decided a medium is.

I suddenly feel uncomfortable in my clothes, or maybe it's my skin. Every year Mom puts aside money so I can have a new first day of school outfit "to make a good impression." She means for the teachers, but I see it as another chance at a first impression with my classmates—a chance for them to see me differently this year. I chose high-waisted jeans and a red T-shirt to compliment my coffee black hair, but I no longer feel the zap of confidence I felt in the store.

"...and they're sending me their new pair."

"What do they look like?"

"I don't know yet, but they said they're glitter. They want me to do an unboxing for Instagram."

It's like I have a sixth sense for him because I lift my head just as Noah rounds the corner. He's wearing shorts and a Franklin football T-shirt, but he's never looked better. His hair is dark and swoopy, his eyes like honey, and he's smiling at me. I wave, and when he waves back all the jitters about outfits and first days vanish. And then he sits down next to Madisen, and I'm brought back to earth.

. . .

Nothing prepares you for the ice-cold dive into an afternoon practice. Nothing. I've been swimming for twelve years, and I still shudder every time I dip my toe in to test the water. Any seasoned swimmer will tell you that's a terrible idea; it's best to just full body plunge into the water and let the shock to your system spring you forward.

Today I'm not alone in my cold water anxiety though. It's five minutes after 2:45, when practice was set to start, and the whole team is hanging around the pool deck drier than an Arizona summer. Only the two freshmen voluntold to get the lane lines in have braved the water, and their shrieks when they jumped in have not inspired bravery in anyone else. Thankfully, Coach Kaitlin is still in the lifeguard office talking to Assistant Coach Avery (who looks half asleep clutching a large travel mug).

"Hey, Kat!" Down by the bleachers, Rachel waves me over to a circle of other seniors stretching. She's saved a spot for me, but when I'm up close I realize no one is actually stretching, they're just making a show of looking like they are. Sam and Isaac, Rachel's twin cousins, aren't even pretending. "Ready for our last season?" she asks.

I've been trying not to think about it all day. But because Rachel couldn't possibly know this is my actual last season swimming—not just in high school—I suck in my cheeks like I've just bitten into a lemon and nod. "What do you think you're swimming?"

She shrugs. "Anything but butterfly."

"I hope you get the 200 butterfly," Sam teases.

"I hope *you* get it!"

I hope I don't get it.

While sticking her tongue out at her cousin, Rachel tries valiantly to get her long blonde ponytail into her swim cap. I used an old trick with conditioner in the locker rooms to get mine on, so watching Rachel do it dry, her hair getting pulled by the silicone, makes me cringe. Rachel and I have been swimming together as long as we've been able to blow bubbles. She's probably my favorite person on the team— despite her neurotic tendencies at swim meets. She always saves me a seat at said meets, swaps homework with me while we wait for our events, and her parents employ me every summer. She's kind of the mom of the team.

Rachel elbows me. "Heard who the new captain is?"

"No, I was going to ask you."

"I bet it's Sean," Isaac says.

"Nah, no way. Sean's too lazy."

"Yeah, but he's good," I point out. Isaac stretches over Rachel to high five me for the support, and Rachel promptly rolls him off her legs.

"Not that good. Weren't you there for our open water race back in July? I smoked him! He wasn't even halfway when I finished."

Sam rolls his eyes. "That's 'cause he likes you."

Rachel scoffs. "No, he doesn't."

"Yes, he does."

She turns to me for confirmation. I bite my lip. It was excruciatingly obvious this summer that Sean has a crush on Rachel. He badgered me and everyone else on the pier to switch days with him so he could work with Rachel and always brought a second water bottle in case she forgot one. Then there was the "race." Rachel is a great swimmer, but Sean can glide through open water like it's no different than a regulation lap pool. So for him to be not even halfway when she finished... Plus there was the big, goofy grin he wore all that day whenever she gloated at him. I don't want to sell Sean out, but what if this is *the moment*? The moment that causes Sean and Rachel to get together. "Yeah, he does."

As Rachel mulls this over, a slow creep of color begins to rise to her cheeks, and pretty soon she's full-on blushing. I can see Sam and Isaac getting ready to tease her, so I hurry to distract them. "I heard Cayla Ashland is off the Glenbrook team."

"Seriously?" they chorus.

I didn't actually hear that (it's more wishful thinking than anything), but seeing Rachel's unwitting smile as she's lost in thought is worth whatever bad karma comes with lying.

The chatter around the pool hushes in a rolling wave. That can only mean the coaches are on their way over. Rachel and I stretch a little more enthusiastically, and Isaac hurries to get his sweatshirt off. Coach Kaitlin loves to force swimmers who aren't ready on time to swim a 200 in whatever they are wearing. She also has buzzed grey hair and a Marine Corp stare that no one wants to be on the receiving end of.

"All right," her voice booms in the echoing pool area, "circle up!" Twenty-five geared-up but slow-moving high schoolers crowd around her (and a coffee-chugging Coach Avery). "Welcome to the season. For those of you that are new, I'm Coach Kaitlin. This," her eyes narrow a bit at her assistant's messy hair and bleach-stained T-shirt, "is Coach Avery." At her name, Coach Avery gives everyone a cheery wave.

"This week we will be working on rosters for next month's meet, and I don't want to hear anything from the peanut gallery about it. Just because you swam something last year doesn't mean you'll swim the same this year."

A few people groan—notably the ones who were swimming sprints last year—and Coach Kaitlin shoots them pointed looks. "Some of you will be swimming the same as last year—" new groans emit from the ones who swam the 200 IM (justified, in my opinion, as the IM is an absolutely hellish event involving all four strokes) "—and I don't want to hear it. You'll swim what you swim because you're good at it."

"Then why the hell was I on the 100 butterfly?" Sam says under his breath. A sophomore I kind of recognize laughs and then quickly bites down on her hand.

"Morning practice is at six, and I mean *in the water* at six, Monday through Thursday. Afternoon practice is in the pool 2:45 to 4:30, Monday through Thursday and every other Friday. If you are sick and won't make practice, you'll need to text Coach Avery. Our first meet is Friday, September 14. If you cannot be at the meet for a *valid* reason, you'll need to let me or Coach Avery know at least a week prior.

"Lastly, I'd like to introduce this year's captain."

Rachel and I share a glance. I quickly scan the crowd to see if Sean is anywhere near the front. People start to part on my left. I stretch onto my toes, as does everyone else, and see Nia Williams emerge. She steps forward to stand beside Coach Avery.

Nia is also a senior. I've known her as acquaintances since middle school. She was the only Black swimmer on our park district team back then and is still the only Black swimmer now. I've only had a handful of conversations with her, but I know exactly why she's been chosen, and now that I think about it, she's the perfect choice. Nia is the embodiment of taking things in stride. Adversity rolls off her like water. She's been our female 200 IM swimmer since sophomore year, and she has absolutely crushed that Herculean event. Never, not once, did she complain about being assigned that beast. Nor did she complain when all the chlorine made a mess of her stunning, natural hair. She just chopped it and held her head high and her chin firm when anyone made a comment. I once heard some of Noah's teammates making fun of her muscular physique when they didn't realize she was in earshot. All she did was walk past and stare them down. That alone shut them up better than anything she could have said or done. She inhales challenge and exhales leadership and maturity.

"This is Nia Williams. She's going to be in charge of handling all uniforms and hunting you down when you're not showing up to practice." Nia stands with her shoulders back and looks as if she's already taking a head count. "If you have an issue, take it to Nia before you take it to us. All right, questions?"

Silence follows, as it does every year after this same speech.

"Then get in your lanes. Warm up with a 300 freestyle."

The lane we swim in during practice is determined by our skill. Usually, the seniors are on the far end and the freshmen are closer to the bleacher end, but there are a few exceptional swimmers that have been in the advanced lanes since their first year—Nia being one of them. She is now in the last lane, the best lane, with only Harry Dehnning. Our lane is the next best, with me, Rachel, Sam, and Isaac all sharing it. Sean is one more over. He's just as good as we are, but our lane is at capacity, and I think even Coach Kaitlin must have noticed the way Sean can't seem to focus when he's close to Rachel.

Sam and Isaac are sitting on the edge of the pool with their toes curled away from the water. Rachel rolls her eyes and jumps between their shoulders, creating a cannonball massive enough to soak both of them and a couple people in the other lane.

"Jesus, Rachel!" they shout. Behind their backs I hold up ten fingers, scoring her jump.

She flips onto her back and kicks more water at the boys. "Come on, slow pokes!" she taunts.

As they stand up and prepare for the cold, I take the chance to jump in and soak them a second time.

Jumping in is not unlike getting pelted by a water balloon in early summer, when the hose tap hasn't been warmed in the sun yet and the water is cold enough to burn. As much as it hurts, I make sure to fully submerge myself. There's nothing worse than doing the slow squat to get your body used to the temperature inch by inch. Once I'm 100 percent under the water, I don't feel cold. I'm pumped. It's like every cell in my body comes alive with the jolt. I spring off the pool floor with a shower of diamond-like water droplets encircling me and turn to check the boys' reaction.

They're not on the pool deck. Before I realize what's happening, two blonde heads disappear under the water, and I'm bear hugged by tsunami waves. When the boys pop up, I'm spluttering.

"Only fair," Sam says.

"You started it," Isaac finishes.

"No," I spit out a mouthful of water. "Rachel started it."

All three of us turn to see Rachel already halfway down the length of the pool and kicking furiously. In fact, everyone has already started the warmup, and we're the only three still standing in the shallow end. Without another word, we all take off.

I push off the bottom of the pool and keep my arms and legs in a tight streamline, enjoying the glide. It's freeing. I'm surrounded by my team, yet there's a solitary peace to being underwater. I can't hear anything but my own breath when I break the surface, and there's nothing to worry about or even focus on besides the rhythmic arm pulls and leg kicks. Swimming is like dancing; it's all about finding the right rhythm and knowing how to adapt when the song changes.

Sam, Isaac, and I are able to catch up, and we wrap up our 300 with everyone else. Nia is surprisingly still on deck and bone dry. She's squatting in front of the whiteboard used to write the practice sets. Coach Avery is beside her, and they are discussing.

"Please no swim/kick/pulls," Sean prays in the lane beside us.

Isaac wipes his fogging goggles with his thumbs. "There are *always* swim/kick/pulls."

Nia stands and the board is visible to all. My shoulders cry out in preemptive soreness seeing brackets around the set and "each stroke" written beside it. That means a 50 swim, a 50 kick, a 50 pull, and a 100 swim for freestyle, breaststroke, butterfly, and backstroke. That's forty laps, and that's just the start. Set two includes a 500 with fins and paddles, and set three is a 200 cool down. Compared to the end of last season, it's a breeze, but there's an air of depression in every lane. Rachel sinks a little lower in the water. Not that we've ever had one, but it seems everyone was hoping for a play-in-the-water day—the kind we had back in toddler swim class.

Nia jumps into her lane, and we are off.

I live for the kicks in the first set. I've always had strong legs and find kicking across the pool just as relaxing as sitting in the sand at Juneway Beach. With my arms on the kickboard and my face in the water, I let my mind wander.

. . .

Nia and Harry, not surprisingly, are finished first. Nia's not the type to run to the locker room, but I can't say the same for the rest of the girls on the team, and there are only three showers. I push myself to go faster, getting so close to Rachel that I can touch her feet. I don't want to be at school even a second longer than I have to be.

As soon as I touch the wall, I rip my goggles off and leap out of the pool. I half stretch—and by that, I mean touching my toes while grabbing my bag so Coach Kaitlin doesn't yell at me—before staking out my claim on a shower. Unfortunately, I'm not alone. When I get to the locker room there's a shower open, but it's the spider shower. We've named its regular occupant Steve the Spider. I don't see him when I pull back the curtain, but that only makes me shower faster. Jade Huberick had a spider jump on her arm once while she was shampooing, and that is honestly my nightmare.

Whatever health my hair regained over the summer feels already destroyed with just one practice. Despite all the conditioner I combed into it beforehand and the near bottle I'd poured into my swim cap, it is starting to feel like straw again. There go my hopes of maybe leaving it down for once this year.

The rest of the team must have finished up because the locker room door opens, and the tight, humid space explodes in noise. I can't pick out a single conversation, but the general theme is the new year. Finished showering, I peek around the curtain and see Rachel waiting for a turn. I wave her over before anyone else notices.

"You are the greatest!"

"No problem."

"Did you get the bad feeling coach is eyeing us for the medley relay?"

"Yeah. I'm hoping she's not going to do to us what she did to Hailey last year." Hailey is a year older than us and was the best freestyle swimmer on the team before she graduated. Last year Coach Kaitlin snatched her up for the medley relay to fill a gap left by a graduated swimmer. Hailey wasn't happy. Last spring the entire girls medley relay team graduated, leaving four of us ripe for the picking.

Rachel shudders. "Just not backstroke. I'm dying to get back to freestyle."

"Well, if she pulls me for the relay, you can have my event," I joke.

"Ha, I wish! Looks like we're getting the side-eye. See you tomorrow?"

"Yep. See you in the morning."

There's another door leading from the showers to the lockers, where it's just as crowded. There's also the added hazard of a soaking wet floor. You would think one of the toilets ruptured with the inch of water slowly creeping down the drain. My flipflops make a *squelch* noise with every step. Other girls have already snagged all the benches and even the sinks to set their clothes on while they change. It will get better as the year goes on and we all start wearing sweats to school, but this first week I know will be a nightmare. Although, I'm not really one to talk with my *still trying* outfit.

I wedge myself in a corner and change as quickly as I can so my clothes won't get wet. As I struggle to pull my jeans up my damp legs, I remember why I always wear leggings or track pants. This sucks.

Getting a spot in front of the mirror is nearly impossible. Mostly freshmen are fighting for a chance to rub off smeared makeup or swipe on new eyeliner. Some are trying to brush out all the knots in their hair. We seniors all have our hair up in buns, and I can't remember the last time I wore makeup to school. I, we, have given up. The battle with chlorine is relentless, and we have thrown down our brushes and mascara and accepted that we will always have our hair up and look like we just rolled out of bed during swim season. Rather than lose an eye elbowing my way into the horde, I squeeze as much water as I can from my hair and thank the universe that it's black and hides the damage well enough.

As quickly as I can, I throw my things in my bag, grab both it and my backpack, and scurry out.

The pool is at the far end of the school by the gym, down a long stretch of hallway before any classrooms or lockers. The wall to my right is floor to ceiling windows letting in afternoon sun that warms and fades the chairs set up along them. In the very last one is Nia.

She is wearing a black Franklin High School Swim T-shirt and a pair of grey joggers. She looks a lot more comfortable than I feel, and I'm unashamedly jealous.

"Hey, Nia."

She lifts her head from looking at her phone.

"Congratulations on making captain. You definitely deserve it."

She smiles, big and warm. "Thanks, Kat. This is going to be a good season."

"Yeah, I hope so." My hair drips cold water down the back of my neck; the rays of sun coming through the windows feel like the biggest tease. I stand awkwardly in front of Nia but can't think of anything else to say. We're not *friends* friends, and I don't know a thing about her outside of swimming. "Um, well, see you at practice."

"In the pool at 2:45," she says, but I'm already down the hall.

• • •

By the time I drop my bags by the door, I'm ready for a bubble bath and trash TV. "Hello?" I say as I step inside. The lights are off, which is unusual because Grandma would normally be in the kitchen around this time. "Grandma?"

No one answers. I turn on every possible light as I make my way to the kitchen. There's a pink Post-it on the fridge that catches my eye.

Kat,

The Way We Thought It Would Be

There are leftovers in the fridge. Sorry I didn't have time to make something special. I hope you had a good first day!
   Mom

The toilet flushes, and I nearly jump out of my skin. I hold my hand to my chest, trying to steady my heart, as Grandma emerges from the bathroom. "You nearly gave me a heart attack!"

Grandma cocks her head. "*Co?*"

I shake my head. I don't know how to say it in Polish and am too lazy to look it up. Grandma waddles past me, back to her spot on the couch with that same book I saw her with this morning. Whatever it is, it must be riveting to get my Grandma, who I've never seen sit for more than twenty minutes, sucked in.

I send Mom a quick *I'm home* text and then dig through the fridge for whatever leftovers she was talking about. Grandma's dumpling soup is there, but I push that out of the way for the weekend's leftover pizza. The black olives, pepperoni, and sausage are calling my name. While I wait for the crust to crisp in the oven, I dig deeper in the fridge for chocolate milk. I'm absolutely starving. I would've eaten the pizza cold, but that would be a dishonor to *Luigi's* and the lovely Italian grandmother that runs the place.

I flip on more lights on my way to the TV. The only one Grandma ever turns on is the lamp in the living room right beside her spot on the couch. I've tried to explain to her before that turning on lights isn't going to make our electric bill astronomical, but she won't hear any of it (partially because I tell her so in a blend of Polish and English). I keep my eye on her as I flip on the TV, but she can't hear it at this volume, and even if she could, she's completely wrapped up in that book. Unfortunately, after a couple rounds of channel flipping, I see there's nothing good on TV at this hour. I don't want to watch the doom and gloom of the news, but I want some kind of noise. The eerie creaks and settling of the house are best when drowned out by Hollywood Housewives.

Mom would kill me if she knew I was eating on the couch, but in eighteen years I have not once spilled or stained anything. Our white couch is as pearly as the day we bought it (but quite worn in). I turn up the volume and scald the roof of my mouth on a huge bite of deliciousness. It's totally worth it.

Too tired to really get sucked into the lives of the too-wealthy-for-their-own-good, I scroll through Instagram to see if anyone is doing anything more interesting. A post by Madisen is at the top of my feed; it's a picture of her coffee table littered with schoolbooks, her slipper-clad feet propped on top of them.

First day and it already feels like we're months in. Thank God for these absolutely adorable slippers from #SoleMate. Use my promo code MADISEN10 for 10% off!

I'm no stranger to Instagram ads (thank you Google for spying on my Internet history), but seeing my friend making one feels off, like the blending of oil and water. These two worlds shouldn't intermix, and yet here they are as one. I peruse the comments, and they're a mix of friends from school and people I don't know at all. I guess that would have to be the case, seeing as the post has already garnered five thousand likes. I don't even know five hundred people, let alone five thousand.

Curious, and definitely not jealous, I click on Madisen's profile to get an idea of just how many followers that dance video has gotten her.

It's unbelievable. Madisen has always been popular online, but almost overnight she's jumped to over 70,000 followers, and the number seems to just keep climbing. I check my own profile, barely scraping 200, and shake my head. Why do I care? I don't know these 70,000 people; why would I care if they don't follow me? I'm not like Madisen.

My profile isn't full of perfectly planned photos that could rival a professional photographer's, they're just swim meets and sunsets. Nothing groundbreaking. Definitely not 70,000 followers worthy. But does it matter? A little part of me says yes; just seeing a number with that many digits makes my heart skip. What would it be like to have that many people think you matter? I can feel the green-eyed monster coming out. *It's just Madisen. She doesn't matt—*

I derail that train immediately. That's not me.

I'm happy for Madisen…or I'm trying to be. Beyond the ads and attention, I know Instagram is more than social media for her—it's art. I've never seen someone work so hard to frame the perfect picture, and they're not all of her or her things either. There are lots of pictures of the three of us girls on her Instagram, for instance. She also does a lot of abstract work in Photoshop that she posts. Even the way she posts is art—creating zigzagging themes and keeping rows to the same color scheme. She deserves this popularity; she works hard for it.

As I'm sitting on her profile, a new post suddenly appears. It's a picture of her and Noah, cuddled up together on her couch under a tie-knot blanket. Madisen is holding a steaming mug, and Noah is holding her. My stomach sinks, but I can't look away. They have such complimentary smiles, Madisen with her high cheekbones, and Noah with the ever-present pink flush to his. They're an attractive couple; there's no denying it.

I put my phone aside and try to get pulled into the story of a mockumentary playing on whatever channel I last left the TV on. But try as I might, my mind is still with my phone. I can make peace with never having the attention of 70,000 strangers, but I can't with never having the attention of Noah Hamilton.

Chapter Three

MY WET HAIR IS still dripping down the back of my neck when I get to Madisen's house. On her porch, I dig through my swim bag for my towel and try to squeeze more water out. Madisen hates when my hair leaves wet spots on her pillows or her couch. I can't blame her; I hate it too, but I'm just used to it.

Before I can ring the bell or text Madisen that I'm here, two red-headed balls of energy come barreling out the front door and nearly take me with them. Ahh, Jack and Charlie. If I had younger brothers, these two are exactly what I would want them to be like. Bold, fearless, and born with mischief in their blood and gold in their hearts. When I broke my wrist a few years ago they signed my cast with pictures of hearts and stick figures farting—if that's not love what is?

"Hey, guys," I call, but they are too busy sprinting across the lawn, around to the back, to notice me. I shake my head and reach for the door, which is a huge mistake because just as my fingers wrap around the handle it is thrown open with such force, I think I may have dislocated my shoulder.

Madisen comes flying out with steam pouring out of her ears. She looks ready to breathe fire. "Did you see them?" she seethes.

"See who?"

"My pain in the ass little brothers." She huffs and her fringe flies up off her forehead.

I shake my head. "No, I just got here." I hear a giggle behind me and try my best to smile innocently.

Madisen storms down the porch steps, her hands clenched into fists, and yells, "I see you Charlie Grace! When you come back in this house you are dead!" I can't see Charlie or his brother, but I hear the two of them scampering away to the backyard.

With her threat declared, Madisen picks up my swim bag and holds the door open for me. "Be glad you're an only child," she says.

I've seen the chaos that Madisen's house can be with five kids running around, but I would take that any day over the silence of being alone. Not wanting to upset her more, I change the subject. "Is Hannah here?" I ask, even though her silver Honda is clearly parked out front.

"Yeah, come on. We're up in my room."

Everything you'd assume about the inside of Madisen's house from seeing the outside is true. There is a foyer bigger than my living room with no purpose other than to be the dumping ground of shoes and backpacks, yet it is decorated with all kinds of expensive looking wood and metal wall art. The dining room has a table long enough to seat my entire extended family, and the living room holds a twelve-seater sectional sofa with an ottoman big enough to be a bed. There's also an ornate fireplace: the kind of fireplace I've seen in Victorian romance movies. It commands the room, stuffed with decorative balls of twine and flameless remote candles. It's entirely useless as Fort Clemens' weather never gets any colder than needing a light jacket, but its uselessness is its purpose. It's a subtle way to tell guests that the Grace family has a lot of money.

Upstairs, each of the Grace children has their own room. The girls' rooms are to the right of the landing and the boys' are to the left along with their parents'. Between these wings is a catwalk that Jack and Charlie are using as the world's steepest Hot Wheels track. Madisen kicks one of the cars over the edge and I hear it dent the living room floor.

Victoria, Madisen's second oldest sister, has her door closed, but I can hear the soft melodies of her piano drifting out from underneath the door. She's no Mozart, but I've always loved listening to her play. I guess their parents feel the same as they were all right with her forgoing college in order to continue making piano cover videos on YouTube. Sarah, the oldest, is the odd man out in that regard. While Victoria has a passion for music and Madisen for photography, Sarah went to school to be an accountant, and as far as I know, she's never indulged in anything frivolous in her life.

Hannah is lying on her stomach on Madisen's bed scrolling on her phone when we come in. She instantly sits up and pats a spot for me beside her. I sit cross-legged and make sure my bun is tight enough that any water in my hair will drip down my shirt and not onto Madisen's sheets. Madisen flops down on my other side and hangs her head over the edge.

If I had to describe Madisen's room in one word it would be Pottery Barn, which is actually two words, I guess. She has one of those impossibly large rooms, like the ones they feature in the magazines, with room for a bed, a dresser and a little seating alcove bathed in sunlight. The walls are a light aquamarine, and there's a fluffy white rug underneath her bed. Each window is adorned with white and blue floral drapes that match the pattern on her reading chair (which is more frequently used to video chat with us). The walls are mostly bare, but there are a few framed pictures on top of her dresser: one of her and Noah from last Christmas, one of all three of us at a football game, and one of a giant technicolor Ferris Wheel at the Ohio State Fair.

"How was practice?" Hannah asks.

"Long," I groan. "My coach has me swimming the 200 medley relay. I'm the freestyler."

"Is that good or bad?"

I shrug. "I mean, it could be worse. I could be swimming the 200 fly."

"That's the really hard one, right?"

"Yeah. That's the one where you have to go up and over like this," I say, mimicking the stroke.

Hannah grimaces. "I hated that one in gym."

"That's why you should've gone to the nurse for *cramps*," Madisen says, using air quotes, "like I did during the swim unit."

"Yeah, I should have." We all know, though, Hannah would never try to pull something like that. If they tell us we need to run a marathon and then dig our own graves out on the football field, Hannah would do it just to keep her head down and her nose out of trouble.

"Have you heard anything from Dina?" I ask.

Hannah purses her lips. "It's definitely happening. Tim called my parents to ask their permission. He and Dina are taking a trip to Redwood National Forest next week, and I think that's where he's going to propose. So does my mom."

Madisen sighs dreamily. "That would be *so* romantic!"

I pat Hannah's knee. "It'll be good."

She shakes her head. "So, what do you guys think about Mrs. Herrera? She's pregnant, right?"

"Oh definitely! I had her last year too, and I overheard her tell…"

Madisen is looking at her phone as she talks, so I catch Hannah's eye subtly. "Are you okay?" I mouth.

"All good," she mouths back. But I can tell it's still eating her up inside.

"…that'll be really cool if she is. We can throw her a baby shower and…"

My phone vibrates in my pocket, and I see it's a text from Hannah. I glance at her, but she's nodding along to Madisen and not meeting my eyes.

It's just not what I thought it would be. I thought next year Dina and I would be hanging out all the time. But now she'll be married and with Tim.

Oh. That makes sense. Hannah's fear of change isn't so much about the newness of adding a family member but losing the one guaranteed friend she'd have next year. Hannah's decision to attend UC Berkeley had a lot to do with the fact that Dina went there and stayed on as an admission's counselor after graduation. As terrified as I am for what's to come next year, at least I'll be rooted in my home. I frown and quickly text back.

You're going to be fine, Han. You're going to make friends so fast.

There's a loud thud against Madisen's closed door that makes all three of us jump. Madisen is quick to her feet and throws open the door in a whirlwind of fury. A Nerf dart just barely misses her head. "Charlie and Jack! I swear to God!" The boys have heard this empty threat enough times to giggle and dash off in the other direction. Madisen chases after them. I take the moment to catch Hannah's attention. Her eyes are a little watery, and I can tell she's far off in the future in her mind. "Hey," I whisper, "it's going to be fine."

"Maybe. I only have two friends now…"

"And how quickly did you make those friends?"

That brings a smile. I nudge her with my elbow at the same time Madisen comes back.

"I hate having brothers," she says with a roll of her eyes.

"We wouldn't know."

"Again, you're lucky. *Anyway*… Do you guys want to see what Penguin sent me?"

"Definitely!" Hannah says with a new enthusiasm.

Madisen pulls a glossy white box from under her bed and sits next to me with it propped on her lap. "This is actually good because you guys can help me with the post I need to make."

Madisen shakes the lid off the box, pulls back a layer of tissue paper, and the first thing I think is *how can I save up for a pair of these*.

"Wow."

"Wow," Hannah echoes.

"Right?" Madisen pulls the right shoe out of the box and slips it onto her foot. It's like watching the duke put the glass slipper on Cinderella; it fits perfectly. They're stark white with a thin line and loop of glitter running along the side that's pure Disney magic. Somehow Penguin Apparel has made shoes that make you look like you're walking on air. When Madisen stands, I realize there's also just a fraction of a heel that makes her calf muscles look even better. "Those look really good on you, Madisen."

"Thanks! They'll look great on you, too. Want to try them on?"

I shake my head. "I wish. Your feet are like three sizes smaller than mine."

I can tell Hannah wants to try them on, but she doesn't say so; she just stares a little longer at them.

"Will you guys help me make a post?"

I shrug, and Hannah nods. "What do we have to do?"

"Just help me get the right angle. I think I want to get a picture by the pool."

Madisen's pool is nothing short of gorgeous. Perfect crystal blue water, black and white mosaic tiles laid around its edge, and a diving board over the twelve-foot-deep end. I remember going to a birthday party once where there was a PVC pipe swimming pool and thinking that was the end all be all of summer luxury—and then I met Madisen. If it was up to me, we'd spend every afternoon out here, but sadly, Hannah and Madisen don't care for swimming as much as I do.

Fully dressed and now wearing both of the Penguin sneakers, Madisen climbs onto the diving board and slowly makes her way to the edge.

"Be careful!" Hannah calls.

Madisen waves her off like she does this all the time. "All right," she says, carefully dropping down to sit with both legs hanging over the water, "can you get a picture with me in the bottom third but without edge of the pool or the back of the diving board?"

Hannah takes out her phone without either of us having to ask her. We both know her later edition has a much better camera than mine. "There's a toy truck in the background. Can you move it, Kat?"

"Sure."

As I scoop up the truck and check with Hannah to make sure I'm not in the shot, I can't help but wonder: when did this become our idea of after-school fun? To be honest, I'd rather be back playing with dolls than taking pictures of each other for social media. Or swimming. I'd definitely rather dive into that beautiful pool than take pictures on its edge. It's like we're here together but we're in separate worlds. Madisen's not really listening to Hannah, and Hannah is busy worrying about the future. Is this fun?

Maybe I'm doing it wrong. I take out my phone and take a picture of my toes curling in the grass. I saw hundreds of Instagram posts like this over the summer. I guess it's kind of fun playing with the filters and seeing just how model-esque I can make my feet appear, but I delete the picture almost immediately. No one wants to see my gross, sweaty feet.

Madisen groans. "All right, this isn't working." Even from here I can see a shy blush on Hannah's cheeks as she starts deleting all the pictures she took. "Kat, do you have any ideas?"

"Um… We can go down to the beach?"

She ponders for a moment. "I like it. Here, help me with this?" I drop the truck and follow Madisen over to Charlie and Jack's swing set. There's a plastic turtle shaped sandbox to the side of it. Madisen grabs the head, and I bend down to get a grip on the tail.

"Why are we moving it?"

"Because—here, this is good—there'll be shadows over there but not here." Madisen pushes the sand into the middle, and for a split second I wonder if she's going to build a sandcastle. But I realize how wrong that idea is when she drops her heel onto the mound she just built. "How about this, Hannah?"

Hannah is about to take another picture but a quick "Wait, wait, wait," from Madisen makes her jump. "No, no. Squat down and rest the phone in the sand. Get an angle coming up towards the sky with the logo in it."

"I…"

I squat down next to Hannah, and together we get something in the camera frame sort of like what Madisen said. Hannah takes the picture, but Madisen asks her to take another, just a hair more to the right.

This is silly. But I guess this is the silliness that gets you free stuff. And the reason why I don't have any free stuff.

I've had enough by the third readjustment and slink away to sit with my feet in the pool. The water isn't ice cold like the school's pool; it's just cold enough to be refreshing on a blazing summer afternoon. I wiggle my toes and watch the ripples spread out all across the water. Eventually, Hannah comes to join me with Madisen behind her. Madisen's eyes are glued to her phone, and her thumbs are sliding and swiping rapidly.

Something about sitting on the edge of Madisen's pool makes me nostalgic. I remember sitting like this back in seventh grade when we thought boys were gross and kissing made you pregnant. I remember standing waist deep in the shallow end the summer before freshman year and feeling so guilty for harboring a secret from my two best friends—that I was in love with Noah Hamilton, and that I was going to ask him out before the summer was over. Then, for maybe a week, I remember feeling equally awful but for an entirely different reason; one I still couldn't tell Hannah or Madisen. It wasn't their problem.

I wonder how many times Noah has been here. More than me? When he and Madisen hang out, is it like this? Together, but each alone in their own head? When we were kids, we could talk about cartoons, animals, even made-up games for hours on end, so why is it so hard to find something to talk about now? Arguably, Hannah and Madisen are two of the people I know best in the world, who know just about everything about me as well, so why is it so quiet? Why is Hannah so worried about making new friends when I'm not going anywhere? Will FaceTiming and texting not be enough? Why is Madisen so focused on people online and not the people in front of her? Is that where she sees her future, with them and not with us? Why am I so concerned with the quiet? Is it because I know that's all I'll have when everyone leaves?

The Way We Thought It Would Be

My phone vibrates again, but this time it's an Instagram notification. Madisen posted the picture we took. She's worked her magic to the extent that I can almost feel the ocean breeze when I look at the picture. She's even edited out the tiniest bit of grass and replaced it with waves. If I hadn't been here when we took the picture, I would've believed she was at Juneway Beach. Apparently, that is exactly what she was going for.

PERFECT day at Juneway! Sun, sand, and of course, Penguin! Check out the link in my profile to get yourself a pair too!

Chapter Four

SCHOOL HAS SOME KIND of rule that practices cannot go past 4:30. Because of this, more often than not, I find myself bumping into Noah on the walk home, and today is no exception. He's ahead of me, wearing a pair of ear buds, no doubt blasting classic rock. His hair is flat with sweat at the base of his neck but is otherwise its usual wavy self. He's wearing that same green hoodie Madisen wore at the beach on the last day of summer break, and I don't know if that makes my heart happy or hurt.

I jog to catch up with him, my bags clanging off rhythm on my back. When I tap his shoulder, he takes both ear buds out and smiles even before he's seen it's me.

"I've got a good one today," he says.

"Oh really? I doubt that."

"Mm-hmm. What do you call someone with no body and no nose?"

"In desperate need of a hospital."

"Nobody knows. Get it? Like, no body…nose." He chuckles to himself.

"Do you crack yourself up?"

"Usually."

"Well, that's good. At least someone is laughing at your jokes."

"Ha ha. How was practice?" Noah reaches like he's about to carry my swim bag for me, but I dodge his hand. He's already got two bags himself, and that would be too much of a tease when I know he's not mine.

Instead, I shift my swim bag higher on my shoulder and hope it will stay there for more than a minute this time. "It was all right. Did I tell you I'm doing the 200 relay?"

"With Rachel and Katie, right?"

"Yeah, and Kennedy."

"What do you think of Kennedy?"

My heart skips a beat. Or maybe it's just completely given out now. Noah probably doesn't, but I recognize this exact question, only with Madisen's name, from right before they started going out. I'm barely okay with him dating one of my best friends. I will not survive him moving on to one of my teammates. At least now I can tell myself that he's not into swimmers, but if he starts dating the girl that's literally me but with curly hair I'll die. Tentatively, I turn it around, "What do you think of her?"

He shrugs. "I don't know. I've got her brother in my P.E. class and he's kind of a jerk. I was curious if she's like that too."

Relief isn't quite what I feel, as I'm still left pining for a guy I most definitely can't have, but it's something close to it. "Kennedy is not a jerk. Not at all. She's actually pretty quiet."

"You would not guess that knowing her brother."

"Is he mean to you?" I try to remember the kids that used to bully Noah. Kennedy's brother would be younger than us, but that wouldn't have made a difference on the playground. Cool was cool and not was not; it didn't matter the age.

"Nah. I just heard him giving Gavin Maccabee a hard time."

I vaguely know Gavin Maccabee, which is saying something because we've all been going to school together for the last thirteen years. He's always been one of the smallest boys in our class, and the sophomore year growth spurt that every boy seemed to hit only made it worse for Gavin. I don't actually know what his voice sounds like because I've never heard him talk. I kind of remember him being really into some kind of collectible card game back in middle school, though. Hearing that Gavin is still getting picked on, even in senior year, makes me clench my teeth. "Did you say something?"

"What?"

"Did you say something? To Kennedy's brother."

"No. I don't know how it is for girls, but guys don't want that. It just makes it worse."

Maybe Noah is speaking from experience, but I can't imagine Gavin wouldn't want to see that someone cares about him. Maybe it is different for boys.

"Where are you going? We live this way," Noah laughs.

"I'm going to Madisen's."

"Oh."

It's one word but it might as well be a novel. I pivot. "What happened?"

"What do you mean?"

I drop my swim bag and my backpack in whoever's front yard we've been tromping through and put my hand on his shoulder. "What happened between you and Madisen?"

He rubs the back of his neck and won't quite meet my eye. "Just a stupid fight."

"About?" I press. I shouldn't get involved, seeing as this is one of my best friends and my other best friend and their relationship, but it's Noah. Dating Madisen or not, there's never been anything Noah hasn't told me. I'm also not afraid to admit that I'm fatally curious to know what kinds of things they fight about.

"I don't even know," he confesses. "It didn't start as a fight, but it ended as one somehow. I'm not really sure what happened, but she said some stuff I didn't like, and I said some things too."

I can feel myself toeing the line of friendly curiosity and prying. It's hard to tell if Noah really doesn't remember what was said or if he doesn't want to tell me. I try not to feel hurt; after all, it is none of my business. "Have you talked to her about it since?"

He shakes his head.

"All right…well, I'm going to get going that way."

"Yeah, all right. Say hi for me."

"I will. And Noah—" He looks right through me to my soul, and I'm warm and soft like caramel inside. "—it'll be all right. Don't worry."

"Yeah, yeah." He half grins and hands me my swim bag. I hoist it and my backpack over my shoulders and continue the trek to Madisen's while Noah turns into our neighborhood.

Sometimes I'm glad I don't have a car, today being one of those days, because the walk gives me time to think. I'm not the biggest fan of Noah and Madisen being a couple, but I don't like the idea of them fighting. If Noah is happy with Madisen, and she with him, then I want it to stay that way. There's no reason all three of us should be lonely and unhappy. Besides, I'll move on…someday.

The Grace home, being the landing place for seven people, has never been quiet, but today it is *loud*. Before I've even reached their driveway, I can hear voices leaking out of the brick walls. Loud, angry voices. Hannah's car is out front, but I think I'll just head home. But maybe Hannah is psychic (or more likely sees me from Madisen's window) because she texts me.

Madisen's mom and Victoria are fighting. Madisen says it's fine. Come up.

I feel incredibly awkward letting myself in to someone else's house--even more so when there's obviously a private conversation happening inside. I'm just about to text Hannah back an excuse to leave when the front door opens, and Mrs. Grace waves me in.

Madisen is a perfect replica of her mother—shoulder length auburn waves, brilliantly blue eyes, and startlingly white teeth. Mrs. Grace is wearing skinny jeans and a leopard print T-shirt under a grey cardigan. She's a stay-at-home mom and a glamorous one. For Madisen's birthday, she used to bring homemade cupcakes piled high with icing to school. They looked professionally made; like something I'd see on Pinterest nowadays. She is every bit the part she portrays herself as in her lifestyle blog *Parenting with Grace*.

"Hi, Mrs. Grace." I shyly duck under her arm holding the screen door open for me.

Mrs. Grace's chest is red, and her exhales are still coming sharply, but she greets me warmly. "Hello, Katarina. Madisen and Hannah are just upstairs. Can I get you anything? Snack? Soda?"

"I'm all right, thanks." Before we both get sucked into small talk, I scamper up the stairs. No sooner does my foot touch the landing before the downstairs erupts in round two of the argument.

"All I'm saying is you need to have a *plan*, Victoria."

"I have a plan, Mom. Music is my plan."

"Music is not going to sustain you! You're not going to be living in this house until you're forty!"

"I don't want to! I don't want to be in this house now!"

"Because it's so terrible having a roof over your head and food to eat? This year, Victoria. I mean it! This year you are either getting a job or you're going to school!"

I guess I was wrong about Madisen's parents supporting Victoria's YouTube career.

Madisen's door cracks open and I slip inside. "That was—"

"Predictable," Madisen finishes. She's sitting on the edge of her bed thumbing through *The Scarlet Letter*. "Victoria told my parents she didn't apply to school again this year."

"Ahh." I can tell Hannah feels as awkward as me. She's sitting up by the pillows, busily studying the pattern in Madisen's duvet.

Madisen continues without prompting. "She's going to be a lifer. I have no doubt in my mind she'll still be living with Mom and Dad when Jack graduates college."

I like Victoria, so I keep my lips pressed together and hope Madisen will drop the subject.

"How was practice?" Hannah asks.

"Great!" Really, it was just all right, but I'm glad at the chance to change topics. "We've got our first meet coming up."

"Home or away? If it's home, I'll come."

"Away. But the one after that is at home."

"You'll do great," Hannah assures me. "I'll come see the next one."

"Thanks." I drop my bags by the door and join them on the bed. They must have been trying to get some homework done because Hannah's copy of *The Scarlet Letter* is also out.

"Do we have a quiz this week?" I direct the question at Madisen because we have English together, but she acts like she doesn't hear me. "Madisen?"

"I don't know. Probably."

"Okay…" I glance at Hannah, but she seems just as confused as I am. I guess the negative energy downstairs is contagious.

A bit awkwardly, we settle into our usual routine of lounging around, scrolling through our phones, and making halfhearted attempts at getting homework done. I peek over the edge of my book at Madisen every once and while, trying to get a gauge on why she's mad. She has her text messages open, and I see Noah's name at the top, but she's not typing. Suddenly she lifts her head, and I'm caught staring. I bite my lip. Now that I'm busted, I want to tell her to just text him; they'll both feel a lot better if she does. But it's still none of my business, so I turn back to my book.

"How many followers do you have on Instagram?"

The question is so unprompted, so out of left field, that it takes me a moment to realize that Madisen even asked it.

"What?"

Her eyes are laser focused on me. "Do you have a lot of followers on Instagram?"

"Umm… I don't know. I can check? Why?"

Madisen shakes her head, a bit of her braid coming undone in the process. "You're never really on Instagram so I was just wondering why. But that makes sense that you don't know."

The way she says *that makes sense* is the same way the women on Hollywood Housewives call their friends a bitch. It's icy, snarky, and a bit underhanded—hinting that there's more she'd like to say. I'm altogether taken aback. Are we in a fight? About Instagram?

Before I can process what just happened, Madisen declares, "I'm bored. Do you guys want to play a game?"

"Sure," Hannah says, a hint of unease in her voice.

I'm still processing what just happened, so having Madisen scoot closer to me makes me feel like a porcupine, ready to fan out my quills for space at a moment's notice.

She feels…off. I can't help but feel that her animosity is directed at me, but maybe I'm just the unwitting target in the storm's wake.

Madisen stretches out her arm, her phone in her hand, and gets us all in view of the camera. It's the first time we've all been squished together on camera and looked uncomfortable. "What kind of game?" I ask. "You're filming it?"

"For Instagram," Madisen meets my eyes through the camera, "Maybe this will get you more followers, Kat."

"I don't—"

Madisen presses record, and I stop talking immediately. "All right," she says in a much more enthusiastic, high energy voice than we've experienced, "Never Have I Ever."

Against my other arm, I can feel Hannah cringe.

"Hannah starts," I interrupt. I want to give her the chance to steer the game away from anything sexual. I've played this game with the swim team enough times to know how quickly it divulges into *Never Have I Ever Done* X *Sexual Act*. Hannah's shoulder relaxes against mine.

"Okay… Never have I ever…faked my period to get out of gym." She shoots Madisen a devilish look.

Madisen and I both hold up a finger because we definitely have done that. Multiple times.

"You go, Kat."

"All right, never have I ever…" and then I grin because I'm about to pull out my secret weapon, my one thing that has gotten everyone I've ever played with, "…gone trick or treating."

"Ugh! You were deprived" Hannah laughs, holding up a finger. Madisen raises one too, but is uncharacteristically quiet, dropping her cheerful act.

"My turn." She turns her whole body and looks right at me, not through the camera but face to face. "Never have I ever slept with my best friend's boyfriend."

At first, I think it's a joke—one I don't understand. I wait for Hannah to laugh and Madisen to break the façade, but Hannah has gone sheet pale, and Madisen is watching me with a firm, set jaw.

"What?"

"I know," Madisen says, icily calm.

"Wait, *what*? Madisen... I didn't... I..."

"Turn the camera off," Hannah says, voice barely above a whisper.

"Madisen, I didn't sleep with Noah." My stomach flips just saying it, and all the blood rushes out of my head.

"Turn the camera off."

"I know about everything." The words are like acid pouring down my throat, burning and drowning me somehow simultaneously.

Hannah reaches for Madisen's phone and manages to tip it out of her grip. It hits the carpet, and there is no other sound in what feels like the entire world. I can hear my heartbeat in my ears. My stomach feels like putty that someone is squeezing tighter and tighter. What just happened?

Very calmly, Madisen slides off her bed to pick up her dropped phone. With her back to us, I can feel Hannah's eyes burning a hole through the side of my head. "Did you?" she asks, barely above a whisper.

"No." I plead with my eyes for her to please believe me. Then I turn to Madisen's back, too afraid to get up and get in front of her. "Madisen, I didn't. I haven't slept with *anybody*." My heart is erratic. "Madisen, I *swear*—"

Madisen pivots, and she has her hand over her mouth. I brace myself for whatever is about to come, the accused facing the noose. But as her hand slips away, I realize it wasn't fury or bitterness she was covering, but a fit of giggles. Tears escape from her eyes, and then she bursts out laughing.

I can't find it in me to do the same.

Hannah is also extremely quiet. Some color is just starting to return to her face.

"Oh my gosh, that was good," Madisen laughs. "Here, look." She holds out her phone and presses play on the video she took, but I'm too floored to look. I feel like I've just been hit by a truck; like a literal rug has been pulled out from under my feet, and I've just hit my head on the concrete.

"I didn't sleep with Noah," I repeat.

"But you like him, don't you?"

I should be knocked silent by the revelation that Madisen knows, that maybe she's always known, but a little bit of my voice creeps out. "He told you?"

"Years ago."

Whatever happens next doesn't matter. Nothing could shatter me more than this. Noah, my kindergarten best friend, my confidante for absolutely everything, divulged the biggest secret of my life to the one person who could never know.

"You like Noah? Madisen's boyfriend?"

Madisen's boyfriend. It stings. Why does Noah belong to Madisen? Why does he have to be hers? Why can't he just be Noah, not Madisen's Noah?

"I did."

"Did you," Hannah swallows hard, "sleep with him?"

"No, I swear I didn't, Hannah. Madisen, I didn't!"

For a long, hard second the two of us stare each other down. I feel on the brink of crying at the absurdity of this. What kind of rumor had someone started? What did Noah say? Madisen shakes her head. "I know you didn't."

If there were any gears left working in my brain, they've all gone flying off into oblivion. "But you just… Why did you…?"

"Because it was funny."

"Funny?"

"I didn't think it was funny," Hannah says.

Madisen rolls her eyes. "Well, it wouldn't have looked real if I told you about it before." She says it so acidly that Hannah's lips form a thin line and seem to seal themselves together.

Not mine, though. "Why did it need to look real? Were you going to post that?"

"Yeah." She says it in such a *well, duh* kind of way that I feel worse about just that one word than about having been accused of sleeping with her boyfriend.

"You can't post that."

"Don't," Hannah echoes.

"It's entertaining," Madisen scoffs.

"It's not true."

"Yeah, it's called a *joke*."

"People aren't going to think it's a joke." I can feel the desperation bubbling up my throat. She wouldn't do that, would she? "Please."

"Oh, come on. No one is going to believe that A) Noah would cheat on me or B) you would do that."

I'm feeling too many things to put words to any of them. I want to ask her why she singled me out. Why would she even do this in the first place? Where did this come from? I'm sick to my stomach, and I want to go home. Convincing Madisen not to post the video doesn't matter as much as getting out of this snake's den and getting somewhere safe.

There's no chance of us going back to homework and sharing internet finds while this accusation hangs in the air. So, with the briefest goodbye glance at Hannah, I scoop up both of my bags and make as quick a dash down the stairs as I'd made up them. It's ironic that not that long ago I'd thought of Madisen's room as a refuge and now I'm running away from it.

Hannah is right on my heels. When we're free on the front lawn, I think she'll say something about how wrong that all was. I'm prepared to make an attempt at laughing it off or excusing what Madisen did as the aftermath of a bad day, but Hannah says nothing. We walk to her car in silence, and when we reach it, we don't hug goodbye. She won't look at me, and because of that I can't look at her. I feel guilty for some reason. Maybe because I have been harboring this secret crush for so long. Is emotionally cheating just as bad as physically doing it? Even though Madisen had said it was a joke and that she knew I didn't and wouldn't have made a move on Noah, I wonder what Hannah is thinking now. After all, why would Madisen randomly make that accusation? And why accuse me? Does Hannah believe it's true or that I'm capable of it? Is that why she isn't talking to me?

Hannah gets into her car and pulls away without any acknowledgment that I'm right beside her. I walk in the street along the curb. My swim bag feels extra heavy and the walk twice as long. I just want to be home. I want to curl up on the couch, finally dry my hair, and I want Mom to be there.

But I know she isn't.

Grandma is in the kitchen, rolling out dough, when I come in. "Hello, Grandma," I say in Polish. But I must not say it loud enough because she doesn't even turn at the sound of the door closing behind me. I don't have the energy to say it again, so I slip past and lock myself in my room. I wish Grandma could hear, I wish she spoke English, but more than anything, I wish I hadn't taken for granted that Mom would always be around to talk to.

I find a new Post-it stuck to the mirror when I go to dry my hair in the bathroom. It's not at all realistic to think Mom could have possibly known what was to happen today when she wrote this, but still I hope to find some kind of sage advice in her note. Instead, it's a grocery list with a little heart at the bottom asking would I mind picking up these few things, love Mom. With the dryer on high, I stare at the stack of unused Post-its and wonder if I should write it all out.

Should I just say Madisen and I got in a fight? Is that even what happened?

There's a sudden clatter in the kitchen. I turn off the blow dryer and hurry to investigate. I don't hear screaming, and I don't see blood. "Grandma, *czy wszystko w porządku?*"

She waves me off. Only then do I see the mountain of flour spilled across the counter and down onto the floor. It looks like a ski slope for ants. As Grandma mutters to herself and tries to scoop up the flour with her hands, I go and search for the broom. We keep it shoved in the back of the linen closet along with the plunger and other miscellaneous cleaning supplies. I glance at Mom's note again and decide not to write one back. There's too much going on in the house. Mom doesn't have time to grocery shop, let alone decipher my problems when she should be eating and sleeping. Besides, she has a day off soon. I can tell her then, in person.

Chapter Five

WHATEVER WEIRDNESS THERE IS between Madisen, Hannah, and I takes a momentary hiatus Saturday at six in the morning when Hannah sends a text in our group chat.

It happened.

She sends a picture too. Dina and Tim are somewhere in the thick of the Redwood Forest, slightly sweaty and glowing. They are both wearing matching plaid shirts, and Dina is sporting a glittering engagement ring on her left hand.

As it's Saturday, and one of the few days I sleep in, my mind is too fuzzy to find the right words. All I can think is *that's a pretty ring*, but I don't think Hannah would appreciate that.

Wow! That ring is gorgeous! Madisen texts.

With a yawn, I rub the sleep from my eyes and regretfully pull myself into a sitting position. Hannah is typing away; I can see the dots appear and disappear over and over. In the meantime, Madisen is sending rapid fire texts.

When is the wedding?

Did she ask you to be a bridesmaid?

Do you know what the colors will be?

In not responding yet, I realize it might look like I'm not interested or not caring, so I rack my sluggish brain to come up with something positive and supportive to say, knowing that Dina's engagement is a mixed bag for Hannah. I wish Tim had waited just a few more hours so I would have had some coffee in me beforehand.

Congratulations, Hannah! It'll be nice to have Dina back for all the wedding planning.

There, that should be good. I should have thought of that earlier. With Dina getting married, there's no doubt she'll be back in Fort Clemens to do a lot of the planning. That has to be a comfort for Hannah, and hopefully Dina will know the right things to say about college next year for her sister.

Yeah, Dina said she's going to come out here for fall and winter break.

Perfect!

Helloooooo?!? Dresses, colors, location??? Do you have a better picture of the ring?

Not wanting to miss details and knowing I won't be able to sleep with my phone vibrating every two seconds, I drag myself out of bed in pursuit of caffeine. I ease my door shut without a sound and tiptoe past Mom's bedroom.

Grandma is already awake and once again reading in her spot on the couch. The dryer is running and so is the dishwasher, which makes me double check that it's only 6 a.m. What time did Grandma get up? Did she even go to bed? On nights with bad weather, Grandma will stay up waiting for Mom to get home. But I don't think it rained yesterday. I glance out the kitchen window. Nope. It's dry as a bone on the patio. That must be a really good book. Maybe I should borrow it when she's done.

I wrestle my hair up into a bun as I wait for the coffee maker to come to life. I check our group chat to see what I've missed. The wedding is New Year's Eve (very cute), Hannah is maid of honor (of course), and there is a close-up picture of Dina's ring. Now I can see it's an oval solitaire on a simple white gold band. It's very Dina—classy but not showy, simple but elegant. Madisen responded with a simple, "Cute!" so clearly, she doesn't like it. But I would never expect Madisen and Dina to have the same tastes.

I love it! I text back. *Let me know when we're going dress shopping ;)*

I don't know that that will be a thing, seeing as it's Dina's wedding and Hannah will probably be looking for her dress with Dina to okay it. But I want to remind Hannah that we'll be with her through this, and I'm also hoping to put the idea of the three of us doing something out there.

It's been three days since the accusation at Madisen's house. She hasn't posted the video, but the three of us also haven't talked. I've been on edge wondering where we all stand with each other, and the only thing that's helped is swimming. For at least three hours a day I'm distracted by the challenges of learning to swim on a relay team and having to depend on three other people, not just myself, in a race. But for the rest of the day, I'm worrying. Madisen hasn't said a word to me in calculus, and although Hannah and I sit together at lunch, we haven't said much more than hello and goodbye to each other.

I feel warm inside at the prospect that this might be the beginning of the return to normalcy. I've had a lot of time to think, and if the accusation never gets brought up again, I can let it go for the sake of our friendship. It's not worth the upset, and Madisen was probably just taking out her frustration with Noah on me. It's not right, but to be fair, she had also been holding onto the secret that I've had a crush on Noah for years. Maybe her frustration with that also got the better of her.

Not wanting to disturb Grandma and her reading, I sneak back to my room with my coffee. In the hall, I catch sight of a Post-it on the bathroom mirror.

I'm off today! Dinner at Blue Whale?

I don't grab a new Post-it, instead scrawling in huge letters under Mom's note, *YES!*

The Blue Whale Bar is a tourist trap but my favorite restaurant in Fort Clemens and anywhere within driving distance. It's a small restaurant on the far end of Juneway Beach with the best beachfront seating. A half dozen tables are scattered in the sand, and on cloudless nights you can see dozens of stars overhead. They also host a nightly competition to guess the exact time of the sunset; the winner gets a free scoop of homemade ice cream. The food is nothing special (besides the Korean barbeque tacos which are other worldly), but any chance I get, that is the place I want to go. I love kicking off my shoes and squishing the sand between my toes, the ocean breeze tussling my hair into endless knots, and the air feeling fresher with every breath. Most importantly, I love Blue Whale because that's the place Mom and I always go when she has a night off.

Despite the early morning wakeup call, I'm aglow, filled with optimism that today is going to be a great day.

Then I get the notification I have been dreading for three days.

"Please no," I pray as I open my phone.

And there it is—bright and bold and undeniable. Madisen posted a video.

My heart leaps into my throat. I open the app and go straight to Madisen's profile. I recognize the three of us sitting on Madisen's bed.

I feel sick. My stomach turns, and I can feel the coffee creeping back up. Why would she post it, especially when I asked her not to? Why now? Why three days later?

Our group chat is silent, and I wonder if Hannah has seen the video yet. It terrifies me to think about it, even though she was there when it was made. It's almost as if having it out on the internet makes it true.

I scroll down to see what Madisen has captioned, but she's left that blank. She just posted the video without a word to say it was a joke. Just a bit below that are the comments. It's like a car crash; I want to look away, but I can't.

Wow, what a terrible friend!

Karma is coming for that bitch.

Soooo sorry, Madisen! Lots of love!

You deserve better.

My coffee sits forgotten on my dresser. I text Madisen separate from our group, in case Hannah hasn't seen the video yet.

You posted the video?

I wait for what feels like an eternity, chewing on my lower lip and pulling at a loose thread on my pillowcase. I can't take it. Why isn't she responding?

Madisen, why did you post that video?

My body is full of frantic, nervous energy. I feel simultaneously like I can run a marathon and like I'm going to throw up. The bubbles appear; she's texting back.

Oh, my God, relax. It's funny.

Who is this Madisen? Hadn't I told her I didn't think it was funny at all?

I don't think it's funny. Can you please take it down?

Instagram is full of videos like this, Kat. Geez, it's a trend right now. Relax.

And to prove her point, she sends me links to about a dozen other Instagram posts. I glance at the captions, and they all have to do with cheating and confronting the supposed cheaters. There's lots of crying, lots of makeup running, and lots of likes. It doesn't make me feel much better. Maybe this is a trend (one I don't understand), but I'm not those other girls. I'm not an influencer, I'm not trendy, I'm Katarina Dobek, and I don't like the idea of anyone seeing me as someone who would sleep with someone else's boyfriend, let alone my best friend's.

But… Who are these people watching this video anyway? I scroll through the comments, just looking at the usernames, and I don't recognize anyone. Does it matter that Madisen's audience of random people thinks this about me? Like Madisen said, anyone that knows me would know that I wouldn't do that, and anyone at Franklin would know Noah wouldn't do that. He and Madisen are the *it* couple; he wouldn't cheat. Not shy Noah Hamilton.

I double check to see if Madisen had tagged anyone, and she hadn't. To all her thousands of followers, I am no one. Is it worth the fight then? A possibly friendship-ending fight? She's been one of my best friends for years. If she says it's not a big deal, then I trust her.

I don't respond to Madisen but return to our group text.

Tell Dina congratulations for us!

As if we hadn't had an entirely separate conversation, Madisen follows my text cheerily.

Yes, please do! And let us know about dress shopping!!!

Mom says we're going to go first week of October to start getting ideas.

Perfect!!!

Can't wait :)

That's that. Madisen says nothing more about the video, and neither do I.

. . .

Mom is still asleep and probably will be until at least noon. She works five p.m. to five a.m., and it's too difficult to reverse her sleep schedule on days off. But that's all right. Today is a Saturday, so I can be up as late as I want and spend as much time as I can with her tonight.

Until then, I need to find something to distract myself so I don't think too much about the video. I try TV but it's too easy to drift away from. Baking helps for a little while, but once I've made the cookie dough, I have twelve-minute increments while they bake with nothing to do but think. Maybe I can run to the park district to swim a few laps before lunch, but then again if we're going to Blue Whale tonight, I'd rather wear my hair down and look a little nicer, and that won't be possible once it gets soaked in chlorine. I'm almost desperate enough to start working on homework before my usual Sunday evening crunch time, but I'm rescued by a text from Noah.

Did you see Madisen's Instagram?

Well, I guess not saved from thinking about the video, but maybe Noah has some perspective that will get me to stop worrying.

Call me.

Grandma is doing laundry in the mudroom as I slip on my flipflops. "I'm going to talk to a friend outside," I tell her.

"*Kto jest na zewnątrz?*" She stretches onto her tiptoes to get a glance out the mudroom window.

I shake my head. "No, no one is outside. I'm going to talk *on the phone* with my friend."

"Ahh." Then she's shooing me out of her way with a flourish of her hands. You have to love Grandma. She never stops, and if you're in her way she'd gladly run you down.

I close the squeaky back door as quietly as I can and grab a seat on one of our lawn chairs as I wait for Noah to call. The sun is warm on my skin, but there's a bit of a breeze this morning warning of autumn days to come. It's almost chilly enough for a sweater. Our shorts days are numbered.

My phone rings, and I pick up before the note can finish. "When does a joke become a dad joke?"

Noah chuckles. "I don't know. When?"

"When it becomes *apparent*."

"That was actually a good one."

"Thank you, thank you."

I wish I could freeze this moment, this tiny minute in all of today where I'm warm in the sun and I have Noah's laughter in my ear. I could sit here, in this time and space, forever. But I know what's coming, and I know it'll be here when I take my next breath—a heavy splash of reality.

"So, did you see Madisen's Instagram post?"

"I did." I don't want to say too much before I know where Noah stands. I especially don't want to freak out about it if he thinks it's funny too.

"I mean," he sighs, and I can practically hear him rubbing the back of his neck, "it's not true."

"Yeah, I know." We both know. Obviously. I can tell Noah is waiting for me to say something about it, but I can't. Especially after Hannah's reaction, I can't give my thoughts until I know where he stands.

"Why do you think she did that?"

"You didn't ask her? She is your girlfriend."

"I just saw it when I texted you."

For a second I smile, we're still Noah and Kat. Noah's first thought was to call me and ask me about it. But as I think about it, my smile begins to fade. Shouldn't Noah have called his girlfriend before his friend? Is it always like this? Were we, Noah and I, giving off vibes that we are something secret behind Madisen's back? Even if she admitted she knows we didn't physically cheat, is Madisen suspicious of emotional cheating? Is that what this is? I would think, if I had a boyfriend, I'd seek comfort and clarity in him before Noah. But then again, in my head, I'd like those two to be one in the same.

"Well…" I hesitate. I'd figured posting the video was for online clout, but maybe there's something more behind it. "I'm not sure. She was kind of upset with me the other day when she made it," I say, thinking back on how Madisen had made a big deal about me not having a large social media following. That felt oddly targeted.

"She was? Shit." My blood runs cold despite the warmth of the sun pouring down on me. Noah never swears. "Kat, I'm sorry."

"Why? Noah, what happened?"

"Well, you see, I said something stupid." My heart begins to race. I sit up straighter in the lawn chair. "Remember I told you we'd had a fight?"

"Yeah…"

"I was upset that she was on her phone—she's always on her phone now, you know—and I said something about it and well, I brought you into it."

"How?"

"I don't know exactly how I said it, but I said something like *Kat is never like this*."

I cover my face with my hand. "Noah, please tell me you didn't say that."

"I don't know if that's exactly what I said, but she said something like *girls are like this* about being on her phone all the time, and I said something about how you're not like that."

I feel an immediate headache. With my thumb I try to massage the pain out of my temple, but it's growing, and it's thunderous. If Madisen knew I had a crush on Noah, and if she was ever at all suspicious of our friendship, Noah may as well have handed her a signed confession saying he cheated with me. "Noah," I groan, "you can't say things like that!"

"Why? What's the matter?"

"Because I'm just your friend! She's your girlfriend! You can't go comparing her to me or any girl for that matter! She's going to think…"

Noah suddenly catches on. "No, but we were never…like that."

Yeah, but you told her.

"You told her about the beach."

It's complete silence on Noah's end. As my words ring in my own ears, my fingers curl into a fist. It's like the gas has been turned on since I found out Noah told Madisen about that day on the beach, and all it's been waiting for is a spark. Well, here it is.

"I have to go," I say and hang up before Noah has a chance to say anything else.

Chapter Six

IT WAS THE SUMMER before high school, and maybe that's why I did it. In every book I've read, every '80s movie I've watched, the summer before high school is the time to make a move. I'd known since seventh grade, when I stopped seeing boys as gross and stupid (and started seeing them as cute and stupid), that I wanted Noah to be my boyfriend.

When we would go to the movies, even with a group, I'd imagine that we were boyfriend and girlfriend and that it was a date. How different could it be? We'd still get to be best friends, except I'd get flowers for Valentine's Day from Noah, and he'd hold my hand when we walked to school. In seventh grade, I knew Noah wasn't looking at girls the way we girls were looking at boys, but by eighth grade, I was hoping every day that he would ask me out.

He didn't. I blamed football and him seeing me too much as his friend. The summer before freshman year, I decided I was going to change that. I took an entire week off from swimming, forcing myself to stay out of the water I was dying to jump into so that my hair wouldn't burn off when I used a straightener. I watched countless YouTube videos to try and learn to curl my hair with one, but after burning three of my fingers, I decided pin-straight hair would have to be as romantic as loose waves.

I labored over my outfit too. I wanted Noah to see me in a new light, and secretly I wanted that whispered, "Wow"—the involuntary gasp in all the love stories when the boy sees the girl as the most beautiful person in the world and you know everything will be perfect after that.

My closet at the time was all athletic shorts and hoodies, so I borrowed something from Mom's. Thinking of it now makes me want to crawl under a rock, but I remember being so full of delusion and dreams that it felt absolutely right to strut down to Juneway Beach in my Mom's pleated lavender skirt, better suited for Easter service than sitting on driftwood. I'd even worn a bit of lip stain. It was a bright pink that I borrowed from Madisen without telling her what I wanted it for. I'd imagined it would leave a mark on Noah's cheek, or even his lips if I was brave enough.

It's funny to remember *that* was what was twisting my stomach into knots. Funny in a sad way. While I waited for Noah to arrive, I was sweating about the potential for my first kiss and whether I could muster up the guts to do it. I never considered things could swing in the opposite direction. Worse still, there were clear signs that my plan was going south, but I ignored all the marked exits without giving them so much as a glance. In my mind, I was going to fly, so there was no need for a parachute.

The first indication that I was not going to leave Juneway Beach a newly made girlfriend, was the complete and total lack of a "Wow" when Noah showed up. In fact, if I remember right, his face was a little screwed up when he saw me, like he'd bitten into a lemon. Who could blame him? His best friend of T-shirts and athletic shorts was suddenly wearing a skirt and someone else's makeup like a kid playing dress up. It should've been a sign that Noah was never going to see me the way I wanted. But I pushed on anyway.

We sat on a driftwood log, and I made the bold move of reaching out to hold his hand. My heart was fluttering in my chest, and when he didn't pull away, it gave me the courage to say all the things I'd practiced in my head.

"We start high school soon."

"Yeah. Are you nervous?"

"Not really. A lot of things will be different, but I'm excited for them."

"The school is so much bigger. I'm afraid I'm going to get lost."

"Don't be. It won't be so bad. Plus…" My tongue stilled. This was it. The leap. "You'll have me."

He smiled so big and warm at me that in that moment you could have told me Noah was the sun, and I would have believed you. "Always."

I'd made the leap, and I'd landed on the tracks I'd been laying out for weeks. All I had to do was keep moving forward. "We've been friends for a really long time."

"Kind of like forever," he teased.

I was too focused on keeping the lines I'd practiced in order to laugh. "I love being your friend, Noah." There it was. L-O-V-E spoken aloud, said straight to Noah's face, just not in the way I was building towards. I was looking ahead to the ocean where the waves were rolling in, turquoise and foamy, but stealing glances at Noah to see if he was freaking out about the *L* word. He didn't seem to mind; his hand was still wrapped around mine. "Actually, I love everything about you." With no signs of panic from Noah, I swallowed the ball of anxiety and dove in. "I guess what I'm trying to say is… I love you, Noah."

The energy rushing through me rivaled lightning. I'd never stood so tall while feeling so vulnerable, and every part of me was electric in anticipation. I'll never forget how it felt to be sitting beside him, beaming, thinking he'd say, "I love you, too." I was high on confidence, 130 percent sure that this was it. This was my *When Harry Met Sally* moment, and the rest of our lives were going to start right then.

In a way, they did. Only not in the way I'd imagined.

Noah's hand slipped away from mine. It wasn't an accident—it was an intentional drawing back and pulling away. That tiny movement obliterated my heart worse than what he said.

"Well, you're my best friend Kat, so of course I love you. But do you mean *love* love? Because… Kat… I—"

"No," I interrupted. I cleared my throat to keep the burn of tears at bay until I was alone. I had to stop him talking. I could know what he was going to say, but I couldn't stand to hear him actually say it. "No, not like that. Just…you know, friends. You mean a lot to me and…I wanted to let you know."

He wrapped his arm around me and gave my shoulders a big bear squeeze. Noah was three years into football and his arm felt much more muscled than I remembered. I hated it. "You mean a lot to me too, Kat. I wouldn't have made it here without you."

Here where? I remember thinking. Here to Juneway Beach, or here to football and popularity and confidence?

"Actually," he continued as I crawled further and further into my skin, "I wanted to talk to you about something."

I remember thinking if he brought up our summer essays I would die right there on the beach. Here I'd just expressed the kind of undying love they write whole books and plays about, and Noah was going to ask for help with summer reading homework.

It wasn't that though. I wish it had been that.

"You know Madisen?"

I mentally blacked out. It was worse than I ever could have imagined. I'd turned over the possibility of rejection a few times in my head, but never, *never*, did I prepare myself for this.

"I know she was dating Matt James for a little bit last year and well, I was wondering if she's over him. You know, has she said anything about it? Because—"

I couldn't have stopped him. The bomb had already dropped, and all that was left to do was prepare for impact.

"—I think I'm going to ask her out."

I cried, but that was later. "Sure," I said. It wasn't really an answer to what he'd asked, but it was enough that I could then fake a family emergency and get away as fast as my legs would take me. I ran the entire way home, Mom's skirt getting ripped up in the wind and sand.

It took Noah two and a half more years to ask Madisen out, but I guess not as long to tell her what happened that day.

Chapter Seven

I'M IN THE KITCHEN making homemade macaroni and cheese (triple cheese and bacon, the way it should always be) when Mom wakes up. She's already dressed and brushed her hair; the only sign that she worked a night shift is the ever-present dark circles under her eyes. I'm still in a funk from my conversation with Noah and Madisen posting the video, but I try and push that aside. It's a rare day off for Mom, and we're going to spend it together—nothing is going to get in the way of that.

"Morning, Mom. Mac and cheese?"

Mom shakes her head. "No thanks. Where's Grandma?"

I point my spoon towards the couch. "She's been reading all day."

"Really?"

"Yeah. Must be a good book to get Grandma to sit down."

Mom agrees and goes to tap Grandma on the shoulder. Not having heard us or Mom's approach, Grandma visibly jumps, and swats at Mom's hand. She starts yelling at Mom about scaring her, and Mom yells back that she should be wearing her hearing aids. It's an age-old battle and one I find it best to stay out of, so I get a bowl and eat quietly at the counter where I'm out of range.

Mom asks Grandma a question in Polish, and when Grandma shakes her head, Mom turns it around on me in English. "Did you get the mail today?"

"Yeah, it's by the fridge."

Mom grabs the pile, and when Grandma sees it, she finally closes her book. There's nothing Grandma loves more than junk mail. She has a letter saved from the Democratic Party (asking for political donations) that she can't read, but it's "signed" by former president Barrack Obama, so it may as well be a Medal of Freedom in her eyes.

She especially loves the coupon clipper books. In the grand scheme of things, all the coupons Grandma has clipped have probably only saved us a few dollars, but Grandma is meticulous about her clipping. She has Ziplock bags in her purse that she uses to organize the coupons into categories. She also has a bag for expired coupons that she pesters me to argue with cashiers to honor. I wish Mom would throw the books out before Grandma sees them, but it makes her happy.

There's one in the mail today. Grandma immediately gets to work with her scissors and her plastic bags.

"Anything for me?" I ask. I'd been accepted to REJC in July, but sort of like waiting on a letter from Hogwarts, I'm always waiting for a last-minute scholarship letter from one of the universities I applied to. Maybe they'd have some extra money they could kick my way, or they'd change their mind about a swimming scholarship.

Mom shakes her head. "No, but there are quite a few bills." She opens one of them and starts biting her lower lip.

"Are they…bad?" I have no idea what our bills usually are (Mom won't tell me), but I get the sense this isn't usual.

"They raised property taxes again." Mom hands the bill to Grandma. Although Grandma can't read it, when she sees the amount due, she starts shaking her head. Then, surprisingly in English, she says, "I go back to work."

Grandma and Grandpa came to America with nothing more than the clothes on their backs and the address of a relative that had already made the journey. Grandma worked as a housekeeper, and Grandpa worked in a factory that made buttons until they'd saved up enough money for their own home. Grandpa died not long after Mom met my dad so when Mom was going to move with Dad to California, Grandma came with them. For a while, Grandma was retired. But when Dad died when I was two, she started working as a housekeeper again. She was working until a few years ago when she hurt herself trying to lift a mattress. After she finished physical therapy, Mom persuaded Grandma to retire permanently.

"You are not working," Mom argues. "You are sixty-eight years old; you're not moving furniture and lugging a vacuum around."

"Mom," I interrupt as Grandma is getting ready to push our couch to show Mom she is a "strong Polish woman," "what if I went back to work. I can go back to my job at the boat rental."

I'm not sure that's true, seeing as summer and tourism season is over, but I would probably get a waitressing job at one of the boardwalk restaurants or something at the park district. But Mom quickly shoots me down. "Katarina, your job is school and to get good grades."

"Yeah, but Mom, I can—"

"No, enough. I'm sorry I brought it up. It's not your job to worry about this."

"I live here too."

Mom snatches the bill back from Grandma and the others from the counter. "It's all fine," she says. "Enough arguing about it. I do not want to fight on my day off. Now I'm going to get a quick snack, and then we are going to go have some fun."

Mom takes all the mail to her room. I share a look with Grandma, but she's right back to couponing with renewed vigor. Maybe it's not so much fun for her but a way she feels she can contribute.

. . .

I sit on Mom's bed as she rifles through her closet for something to wear. Nightlife for Mom consists of wearing scrubs and getting her shoes stained with bodily fluids (her words, not mine), so she's having a bit of a crisis. I see the lavender skirt zip by on a hanger, and I duck my head.

I've received a few texts from classmates asking about the video they saw on Madisen's Instagram, and not wanting to sour the night, I turned off my phone. It's currently lying on my bed where I won't be tempted to see if Madisen has taken the video down or if Noah has texted me.

"What about this?" Mom asks, holding up a white blouse with orange butterflies on it.

"I like that one," I say, remembering her wearing it for my eighth-grade graduation. It flatters her dark bobbed hair.

"Yeah?" Mom looks unsure, and I don't blame her. It's hard to break out of your daily uniform. I'm wearing a scarlet, bell-sleeved blouse and jean shorts, but my joggers are calling out to me. When you live in comfy clothes, jeans feel like a cruel medieval design.

"That sundress looks nice, too." It's jade green with tiny white daisy print and a layer of ruffles on the hem.

"Can I wear sneakers with this? I want to wear my arch supports tonight."

"Do you have non-work white ones?"

"Yeah."

"Then yeah, wear those."

I opt for a pair of cork wedges that I've had for four years and have probably only worn four times. We'll be doing a little walking tonight, but since I'm already dressed up, I figure why not. Plus, they'll be much easier to slip off in the sand than anything that ties.

We ask Grandma once more before we leave if she'd like to come with. We know the answer will be no—it's always no—but we ask anyway. When she says no once again, Mom and I grab our purses and head out.

It's only four p.m. but already the sun is beginning to set and the sky burns pink and gold on the horizon. Autumn is here with coastal warmth in the air.

"How has the first month been?"

"School or swimming?"

"Both."

"It's all right," I say, because I can't think of a better way to describe it. The ease of the first week passed all too quickly and now it feels like summer didn't happen at all. It feels like we're hurtling towards graduation at breakneck speed. Every teacher reminds us that in college the expectations will be higher and that this and that won't be acceptable, and all I can think about is how I won't be there. But that's not something I'd tell Mom, especially now, knowing our bills are getting worse.

"Just all right?" Mom reaches over for my hand and rubs circles on the back of it with her thumb. "How's the medley relay?"

"Better. I'm getting used to it now, and the team is really good."

"Rachel is on it, right?" Mom has liked Rachel since an elementary school swim meet where I forgot my goggles and she loaned me hers. I have to give Mom credit too. Even with the thousand things on her plate, she's still managed to keep a part of her memory saved for the things important to me.

"Yeah, Rachel has backstroke, Kennedy has breaststroke, and Katie butterfly."

"Poor Katie."

"No, she likes it. She's been swimming it for years."

"Trooper."

That too. That Mom knows how I feel about butterfly and empathizes. It makes me feel even more guilty that I'm not working and contributing.

It's still a little early for dinner, so instead of heading straight to the beach and Blue Whale, we make our way across the street to Fort Clemens' downtown. I use the word *downtown* loosely because really it is two blocks of shops mostly aimed at tourists. The buildings are all white brick with hand-painted signs jutting out over the sidewalks—the only sidewalks in all of old Fort Clemens. The stores are generally long and narrow and sell handcrafted goods, the kinds of things you'd find on Etsy. With tourist season over, most have switched to off-season hours and are either closed for the night or getting ready to. Mom and I zigzag between the ones with their doors still open, looking at dresses, beaded jewelry, and a plethora of seashell-themed home décor.

"Oh, look at this, Kata," Mom calls from the other side of Schuster Sisters' Boutique. She's holding up a gold necklace, but I can't make out what's hanging from it until it's in my hand. It's a very simplistic design: a gold chain with a gold pendant about the size of a dime in the shape of a circle with a single wave flowing across it. "Is it more of a surfing necklace?" Mom asks. "I thought it could be swimming."

I love it. It's simple, it's me, and it would remind me of Mom whenever I wore it. But I don't tell Mom this because although it's a simple necklace, it will cost at least $40 with tax. "It's nice," I say instead.

I can feel Mom trying to read my face. "Would you wear it?"

Yes.

"I don't need anything," I say and hang the necklace back on its display.

"Well, no one *needs* a necklace, but do you want it?"

I shake my head. "It's all right. Thank you, though." Then I slip back to the other side of store so I don't feel worse.

As I'm running my fingers over a loose knit sweater, Mom rejoins me. "Ready to eat?"

"Sure. Wait, what's that?"

Mom is holding a small grey box not-so-secretly in her hand. She smiles guiltily and opens it to show me the wave necklace set on a bed of tissue paper. "Mom, you didn't have to get me anything." I want to tell her to return it, to save the money for bills, but I don't want to upset her.

Mom shakes her head and hands me the box to hold while she secures the necklace around my neck. "I didn't have to, but I wanted to. It looks beautiful on you."

I brush my thumb over the pendant, feeling every sentiment under the sun.

As we head toward the beach, the necklace seems to be getting heavier and heavier. Each bump against my chest feels like a stone. Why would Mom buy me this when we're struggling? Is it because I heard and she doesn't want me to worry? I'm eighteen. I understand, and more than that, I can help. Why won't she let me?

"What's new, honey? How are Hannah and Madisen?"

My heart deflates. "They're fine."

"And Noah?"

"He's all right." Mom squeezes my hand, so I add, "He's going to UCLA next year."

"That's fantastic! Good for him."

I don't tell her that he's going there because Madisen is. Or that he told Madisen about my confession of love. Or that I confessed my love to Noah. Or that I love Noah. Or that Madisen accused me of sleeping with Noah.

When we reach the sand, I pull off my sandals, but I don't feel the usual sense of ease as my toes sink into the still-warm sand. The beach is dotted with light from the restaurants, a stark contrast to the inky black ocean cutting a line along the shore. Even though I can't see them, I can hear the waves rolling in against the breakwaters. We step around abandoned sandcastles and approach Blue Whale Bar from the back. The tables out in the sand are mostly empty, and the hostess seats us at one close enough to the ocean to smell the salt on the air but far enough back for the sand to still be soft and dry.

I pore over the menu for the first time in years. My usual is $12. There's a chicken fingers basket that's only $6, but I'm not sure they'll let me order off the kid's menu.

Mom puts her menu down. I can feel her eyes on me, so I pretend to be consumed reading the entrees.

"Kat, look at me."

I do, but I fear she can see my anxiety written all over my face.

"Don't worry about money." I duck my head—busted. "Don't worry about bills or anything like that. I'm sorry you heard earlier. I don't want you to worry, and I especially don't want you to not get what you want for dinner. This is our day, and I want you to be happy."

"Okay, Mom."

"Is there something else bothering you?"

I almost tell her. The words are there just behind my lips, but when I look at Mom, I don't just see my mom. I see the woman who lost her husband and best friend but kept going for two-year-old me, the woman who works twelve-hour nights to keep us in our house and still finds a way to support my swimming. There's a mountain of worries on her shoulders; I can't add mine.

"No, I'm all good." I put my menu down as well, hoping to prove to her that I'm all right now. "Hannah's sister got engaged," I say, knowing we'll spend the night wondering about the wedding, maybe reminiscing about Mom's and Dad's, but not worrying.

Chapter Eight

IT'S OUR FIRST HOME swim meet, and true to her word, Hannah is up in the bleachers with other friends and family cheering on Franklin. She's dressed in layers and has already shed her sweater and kicked off her shoes. I'd warned her the pool deck can feel like a greenhouse, especially during meets when there are so many extra people around.

I'd texted both Hannah and Madisen that my race wouldn't be until the latter half of the meet, but when I surveilled the pool deck a few hours in, I only found Hannah. Madisen is usually hit or miss with swim meets, but today it feels more intentional. Is she mad at me? Really, it should be the opposite. After giving it some more thought, I don't care what Noah said. That's between the two of them, and if she wants to be mad at anyone, she should be mad at him, whereas I have every right to be mad at her for putting that lie out on the internet.

I've been tiptoeing around the team, wondering who has seen the video and who will be the first to ask me about it, but so far no one has said a word about it. Hopefully, that's because anyone who's seen it knows how ridiculous the accusation is.

There are still a dozen or so events before ours, so I tell the girls I'm going to say hi to my friend for a minute.

"Okay, but hurry," Rachel says. She's been standing for the last twenty minutes and already has her cap on. Katie rolls her eyes and winks at me. We all know how Rachel gets at meets.

The team is camped out in the hallway between the gym and the classrooms, so when I enter the pool deck it's like stepping off a plane into a tropical climate. All I feel is warmth and water in the air and on the ground.

Hannah has a book open on her lap and her phone beside her on the bench. I always text her before my race because when we all have our hair up in caps, and we're all wearing the same scarlet swimsuit, it can be difficult to tell us apart. She's wearing our school's colors in the form of a red T-shirt and white shorts, probably the most subtle of anyone on the bleachers what with all the moms in their custom "Franklin Swim Mom" shirts.

"Hey there!" I shout over the noise of the current race. When eight people are cutting through the water at the same time, the splashing can be deafening.

"Hey!" She pushes her glasses up her nose and closes her book. "When is your race?"

"Not for a few more. Thanks for coming."

"Of course!"

"You know you're welcome to come sit with us."

She shakes her head. "That's okay. I haven't finished the chapters for English yet." She holds up her book, *The Scarlet Letter*.

That's the best part about being on the swim team as compared to any other sport—the down time. I'd finished all my calculus homework and read this week's (and last week's) assigned chapters in *The Scarlet Letter* all before even getting into the pool. "It might be quieter," I say.

"No, it's okay. Thank you, though."

For a moment I worry Hannah is still hesitant around me after what happened at Madisen's house, but I quickly realize she's probably more uncomfortable sitting with the swim team than sitting here alone. There are too many people and too many *loud* people. We can be a lot sometimes since we've all been swimming together since we were five.

"No worries. Well, do you want to do something after? Maybe get lunch?" Usually, the team goes together to get a late lunch, but I'd rather go with Hannah. We haven't really talked since she told us Dina got engaged.

"I can't. We're flying out tonight to go see Dina, and I haven't packed yet."

"Oh, okay. Well, I'll come say goodbye after at least." It's not unusual for Hannah's family to take short weekend trips out to Berkeley, but I still feel disappointed. "I should probably get back. We're up in a few."

"Good luck!"

As I'm heading back, the last racers are just getting out of the pool, and I catch up to Sam and Isaac. "How'd it go?" I ask, ducking under Sam's arm holding the door open for us.

"First and second," Sam beams. "I was first, of course."

"Barely," Isaac grumbles.

"By at least a second."

"Half a second."

"Firstborn, first place."

"First to go bald."

"Oh, my *God*," Rachel groans as we join the circle. "You guys are so irritating."

Ignoring her, Sam asks, "Why are you standing? Aren't there like six more races before the medley?"

Rachel glares at him.

"What are we working on?" Isaac asks, dripping onto Kennedy's book. She swats him away and dabs at the wet spots with her shirt.

"Chemistry."

He whistles. "Can't help you there."

"We're in idiot science," Sam says.

"Idiot science?"

"Physical science," they say in unison.

"So, like physics?"

"Oh, no." Isaac laughs.

"Like the earth is round, plants make their own food, fifth-grade science," Sam says.

"You guys are smarter than that."

"Yes, but we don't care to apply ourselves."

"As our dad says."

"The guy who scoops ice cream for a living."

Rachel clears her throat. "The guy who owns a chain of successful ice cream shops across California."

"Details, details."

Not wanting to get involved, I busy myself on my phone. One of the sophomores has her hair up in a braided bun that I want to copy one day, so I try and find a tutorial on Pinterest. As I'm falling down a rabbit hole, I somehow find myself on Instagram, and not long after, I'm on Madisen's profile. She's since posted a few new pictures, but I scroll down to where the video should be. It's still there with close to eight thousand likes now and a couple hundred comments.

"All right, kids," Rachel says, shaking me out of my thoughts. "Let's get ready."

If Rachel is getting ready to go, we still have a good ten minutes before our race. There's probably enough time for a bathroom break, but Rachel is already bouncing from foot to foot, so begrudgingly, Katie, Kennedy, and I stand too. I send Hannah a quick text letting her know our race is coming up and follow the girls out onto the pool deck.

Once we're there, lined up at the blocks behind the current race, Rachel's nervous energy rubs off on me. As the freestyle swimmer, I'm the last in our relay, and I'm supposed to be the fastest. I did well last year, even placed first in a few meets, but am I fast enough to hold up the team? We are all counting on each other to be the fastest, to give the next girl a little jump ahead of the other teams. If Rachel, Kennedy, and Katie all give me a few seconds ahead of the other teams, and I mess it up…they'll probably forgive me but I'll know we would have had it if it wasn't for me.

We are squished in the crowd of swimmers, coaches, and timers behind the blocks. Someone keeps elbowing me in the ribs, and the muffled voice over the intercom announcing the races can barely be heard over the chatter.

"Was that us?" Kennedy yells. She is still trying to tuck all of her curls into her cap.

"Yeah, this is us!" Rachel grabs my elbow and Katie's wrist and pulls us to the blocks.

"Ow. Ow!"

The space behind the blocks is always extra crowded for the relays. There are four swimmers per block plus coaches, timers, and friends. I've found that the relays tend to draw more of an audience because the lead can change with every swimmer.

Katie is up first. The order is butterfly, backstroke, breaststroke, then freestyle; Katie, Rachel, Kennedy, me. We line up in that order, each squeezing the shoulder of the person in front of us. It's our practice ritual, a little *you got this* encouragement.

Between the murmurings of the last race and the start of ours, a hush falls over the water. It isn't much and only noticeable to the swimmers on the block and us right behind—a breath before the jump, a crackle of electricity in the air.

BEEP!

Katie dives perfectly, flowing from a torpedo streamline to strong butterfly kicks that propel her a little more than halfway across the pool without a breath. Rachel pencil dives in, waiting in the water with her hands on the block because the second Katie touches the wall, she's taking off.

"Oh no," Kennedy breathes. She turns and nudges me to look over to our left. "Looks like Ashland is on the medley team this year too."

Down at the furthest lane, all in emerald suits, is the Glenbrook High School team. Last in line is Cayla Ashland. She's a senior like us, and the rumor last year was that her GPA was so low she wasn't going to be allowed on the team this year. That was fine with us as Cayla was practically built to be a freestyler. She is thin and tall, a string bean that can glide through the water better than a fish. Seeing her should make me nervous, but actually it fuels me. We are *not* losing to Glenbrook.

"Just give me a little lead," I say.

"You'll have it."

Katie is about a hand's length ahead of the next fastest swimmer as they're making the return lap. Rachel pulls up on the block. Then, just as Katie's fingers brush the wall, she dives backwards, cascading into the water in a beautiful arch, and kicks hard beneath the surface. She makes it almost the full length of the pool before she's up for a breath. When she flip turns at the opposite wall, Kennedy climbs up onto the block.

I put my goggles on as Kennedy dives in and Rachel pulls herself out of the pool. We don't say anything to each other for fear of jinxing the small but significant lead we have. I climb up onto the block, and instantly I'm about ten degrees colder, either from escaping the wall of bodies on deck or because my body is preparing for the chilly water below. My cap is on tight. I smoosh my goggles onto my eyes even tighter and adjust the straps on my one piece. On either side of me, the other girls are doing the same. All the way to my left Cayla Ashland is doing some last-minute arm circles. She must feel my eyes on her because she turns and smirks in my direction. I shake my head. If she thinks that's going to intimidate me, she better step up her game.

Kennedy is on the return lap. I get down into position with my fingers gripping the edge of the block. My heart is pounding, and I take deep breaths, trying to get my breathing regular and ready for the race. She's close, just three more strokes. Behind me, Rachel and Katie are screaming, but so is every other team, and it's all just a blur of noise I drown out. It doesn't matter. I'm just waiting for Kennedy to touch the wall. As soon as she does—

I push off from the block and for a brief moment, I am flying. Then my fingers cut through the water, and I plunge in headfirst. Thankfully, my goggles stay on just right, and I'm able to stay in a tight streamline without needing to adjust. The temptation to look over and see if anyone else is gaining on me is strong, but I don't for fear of breaking the glide. When my lungs start asking for air, and I can feel myself slowing down, I start to butterfly kick, trying to get as many yards as I can before breaking the surface.

The first breath is crisp. My legs are two flippers going at top speed and my arms cut through the water rhythmically. The wall is coming up. The black line at the bottom of the pool is about to become a cross. I take one more pull with my right hand, one more breath, and then I flip. My feet touch the wall, and I spring off. To my left I catch sight of the bubbles of the other girl who also just flip turned. I'm not sure where I am in the race, but I think I'm first or close, so I kick it into high gear (pun intended).

Every time I take a breath it is a roar above the surface. I can just make out Rachel screaming, "You've got it! You've got it!" I take that to mean I'm leading the pack, and I decide to forego breathing the rest of the way. I'm all arms and propeller feet, forcing the water out of my way.

My fingers jam into the wall.

I don't care that I might have just broken my fingers. I yank off my goggles and look over at the board, looking for the winning lane. And there it is. A big, glowing red lane three—our lane. We crushed it!

I don't climb out of the pool so much as I'm pulled out by the girls. Rachel is beaming, Katie claps me on the shoulder, and Kennedy is already off sharing the news with her boyfriend.

"Looks like we've got a good team this year," Coach Kaitlin says as we pass her chair on the deck. We all thank her and eagerly rush back to the hallway to share the win with the rest of the team.

Isaac and Sam look at us expectantly (and also a little guiltily because it appears they got our nice, dry towels all wet). Rachel tries to psych them out at first, but she can't wipe the grin from her face. "We won!" she gloats, putting her hands on Isaac's shoulder and jumping like a kangaroo.

"Nice job!" they chorus. "Welcome to the winner's circle," Sam adds with a smirk in his brother's direction.

Katie interrupts before they start fighting again. "*And* Kat beat Ashland!"

The boys' eyes grow huge. "Ashland is back? Wow, Kat, fantastic!"

I shake my head. "It was a team effort. Rachel, Katie, and Kennedy got me a really good lead on her."

"Hardly," Rachel snorts.

"Hey, guys." Nia comes over decked out in all the Franklin High swim gear. The 200 IM is one of the last events, so Nia has been posted up by the coaches most of the meet, keeping track of how we were doing. It's about 95 degrees in the pool area, but that hasn't stopped her from wearing our team hoodie. "Great job in the medley!"

"Thanks, Nia," I answer for the group. "Are you ready for yours?"

"Yeah, I heard St. Benedict's team doesn't have a female 200 IMer so that'll be—"

Kennedy rushes back to our group, nearly slipping on a puddle and knocking herself out. "Hey, let's get a picture of the team!" She thrusts her phone out. "Nia, do you mind?"

But as soon as Kennedy said picture, Nia turned on her heel.

Katie's eyebrows furrow. "What's up her butt?"

"We'll take it for you," Sam offers.

We find a spot on the wall without a glare from the windows, right below the word *Franklin* in the school's mural, and the four of us stack ourselves two high and two low. After we get a nice photo, Rachel calls for a *Charlie's Angels* pose. We stand back-to-back with our fingers pointed like guns and the most serious faces we can manage while Sam and Isaac clown around on the other side of the camera. Kennedy reaches for her phone, and we circle up to approve the photos.

"Guys! Did you take any of *us*?"

Rachel lunges at the boys. Isaac ducks out of the way, but Sam gets a good swat on the back of the head.

There are about fifty selfies of Sam and Isaac in Kennedy's phone now, but mixed in there are a few of us. "Don't delete these," I whisper to Kennedy. "I know someone on the yearbook committee, and I bet we can ask her to blow one of these up on a whole page."

She grins. "I'll send the worst ones to you."

Even though we are done swimming for the day, we stay for the entire meet. We want to support our team, and it is also mandatory that we do. We pull on team sweatpants and shirts, trying to warm up from the icy water, but we soak through them now that our towels are wet rags, thanks to Sam and Isaac.

"What do you guys think about getting shirts?" Rachel asks, holding her phone out to us. On a custom shirt website, she's already designed a set of four pullovers in our school's scarlet and white with our stroke on the back in big, chunky letters.

"I love them!" I say, trying not to look at the price.

Katie squints at them. "Can we do white with red letters? I hate red."

Rachel gestures to the huge wet mark on the front of her shirt. "It has to be red with white. I don't want everyone seeing my nipples when I soak through these." As the biggest chested of us, Rachel has the authority there, so we agree (although Katie is still a little sour).

"We'll have them by next meet," Rachel says, placing the order.

Kennedy is already pulling cash out of her swim bag. "What do we owe you?"

Thankfully, Rachel waves her off. "Give it to me when we get them. It'll be forty each."

I breathe a sigh of relief; at least I have more time to save up. I can ask Mom for the money as an early birthday present or dig into my college savings a little.

All four of us jump on Instagram to post the pictures. Katie and Kennedy are classy and choose our normal picture, but Rachel and I go with the *Charlie's Angels* one.

#squadgoals Here's to first place at the first home meet of the season! I caption it.

As I'm about to close out of the app, something on my profile catches my eye. I blink twice to make sure what I see is real.

2.7K Followers

My followers have shot up from just a few hundred to almost three thousand. Frantically, I scroll through the new names, but I don't recognize any of them. Can this really all be from Madisen's video? I jump over to her profile, and her follower count is astronomically high. I guess Madisen was at least right about that; it seems like this is some new Instagram trend and she hit on it when it was hot.

Even though I told myself I wouldn't, curiosity gets the better of me, and I read the first few comments on Madisen's video. They are brutal. I can feel the blood rush out of my face. The overall theme is that I am a whore and Madisen deserves better. Are these commenters the same people now following me? I quickly memorize the username of one of the more vicious commenters and search my list of followers for it. Thankfully, it's not there.

"Last event," Sam announces.

Rachel nudges me. "Let's go watch."

"Why?"

She shrugs. "Support?"

This is new. I glance at the roster taped on the wall to see what race this is. It's the 200 IM for the boys. *Ahh.*

"This wouldn't have anything to do with Sean would it?" I wiggle my eyebrows, and Rachel blushes.

"Just come on," she grumbles.

"Hold on," I laugh.

I text Madisen quickly. *Hey, have you seen some of the comments on your video? They're pretty bad.*

I barely hit send before Rachel is yanking me to the side of the pool by my elbow. Sean is in the nearest lane, and Rachel pulls us so close our toes are practically in the water.

Although Sean is probably one of the lazier guys on the team (always late, last one in the water, etc.), he is a great swimmer. Endurance is his forte, and for a 200 IM you need a *ton* of it. While he starts off the race in the middle of the pack, by the last lap Sean hasn't slowed a bit, and that gets him second place. Not bad for the second meet of the season. Sean seems to think so too because he comes out of the pool all smiles. It doesn't escape me that one of those smiles is directed at Rachel.

Coach Kaitlin and Coach Avery herd the team over to our section of the bleachers, and we all stand shoulder to shoulder. The early event swimmers are already bone dry and Nia and Sean are bundled in towels. I stand on my toes to try and see if Hannah is still around, but there are too many tall people to see around. As the coaches give their post-meet talk, all I can think about is if Madisen replied to my text.

When we are dismissed, everyone heads back to the hallway to gather their gear, but I stay back and look for Hannah. The bleacher crowd is also packing up their snacks, books, and iPads. I step over someone's little siblings' spilled crayons and dodge elbows as I make my way against the crowd. Hannah is already packed up, but she's still sitting on the bleachers waiting for me. "Sorry it took a minute. We had a post-meet talk."

"It's okay. I've got to get going, but… I wanted to talk to you about something."

I swallow hard. "Okay."

Hannah tucks her hands into the sleeves of her sweater. "It's about Dina's wedding."

If my breath of relief is audible, Hannah doesn't let on.

"I know we were planning on going dress shopping in a week, but… Well, I was wondering if maybe…maybe you'd want to help me and Dina make the invitations later instead?"

"I don't mind doing both," I assure her. "I don't have a sister, so this is all new and fun for me."

Hannah pushes her glasses up her nose with her fist bunched up in her sleeve. "I was thinking maybe just

Madisen and I would go dress shopping. Then it can be just you and me for the invitations…and Dina."

"Is this because of what happened at Madisen's house? Hannah, you know it's not true right?"

"I know," she says, but her gaze is now on her shoes. "But I don't want to get in the middle."

"There's nothing to get in the middle of though. We're still talking." I think about the text I'd sent Madisen. Did she respond? Maybe we aren't talking.

"I just think it would be better if we don't all go together. I think it would be easier."

I feel like I've been sucker punched. "Then why don't you ask her to go another day?"

Hannah fidgets with her sleeve again. I can practically feel her melting beside me, and I hate that I feel like a giant watching her at my feet. I say, "All right, that's fine."

"Thanks, Kat."

I nod, but I feel completely numb. The heat of the pool deck can't seem to penetrate my bubble. "Have a safe flight." I'm standing before I realize it. "Say hi to Dina."

"I will. Good job today."

"Thanks." It's a hollow sentiment, like a drug store greeting card.

The hallway is mostly cleared out when I get there, but there are a few people still lazing about, and my bag is there, untouched. I shoulder it and find my phone. I'm almost afraid to see if Madisen texted back, and I'm not sure if it would be better if she did or didn't. But sure enough, there's a text.

Just ignore it.

I frown. How can I ignore what people are saying about me—the *untrue* things people are saying about me? Especially when it could all stop if Madisen would just take down the post.

Madisen, take down the—

91

Through the hall windows, I have a view of the school's parking lot, and I see Hannah getting into her car. I erase what I typed. If Hannah is already thinking Madisen and I can't stand each other, that text might assure it, and I can't put Hannah in the middle. Especially if it means I'll only have half of Hannah's friendship. While I hate that the video is out there, I'd rather that than lose Hannah completely. Instead, I text Mom that I'm on my way home.

Chapter Nine

ON THE SATURDAY I should have been going with Hannah, her mom, and Madisen to look at bridesmaid and mother-of-the-bride dresses, I woke up to two upsetting notes. The first was a Post-it on the bathroom mirror from Mom.

Have fun dress shopping today! Send me pictures!

In the week since the swim meet, I haven't told Mom that I'd been uninvited to the shopping trip. It's one more thing that I don't want to add to her plate, and really, in the grand scheme of life, it's not that big of a deal. Although when I saw that note on the mirror, it was hard to remind myself that.

The second note came in the form of a text just as I was settling down with my cup of coffee and convincing myself I could enjoy the day without my friends. It was from Noah.

I'm sorry I told Madisen. Please talk to me.

For five days I've succeeded at avoiding Noah. Every afternoon after practice I either made sure to bolt out of the pool and run home still in my suit, or else I hung back so long that even the janitor had gone home. Noah hadn't texted or called, but I figured he knew I was avoiding him, and this text confirms it.

I haven't responded to either of the two notes. At least with Mom's I have time, but every passing minute I don't respond to Noah, I can feel the divide between us growing.

Truth be told, I'm not as mad at him as I was before. Without knowing or wanting to know the details, I accept that there is some situation out there where it would have been necessary for Noah to tell Madisen about my profession of love and how he rejected me. If she had any suspicion at all, that would've been reason enough to tell her that he had his chance with me, and he didn't want it. But now I'm in this foreign territory where for once in my life I don't know how to talk to Noah.

My phone is sitting open on the arm of the couch as I sip my coffee. Maybe if I stare hard enough at the TV the words will come to me. Although those words might be in Spanish as my channel flipping stopped on a *telenovela*.

"No English?" Grandma asks from the other side of the couch.

"No English," I confirm.

She seems very confused. Perhaps in Grandma's mind there are only two languages: Polish—the one she speaks—and English—the one everyone else speaks.

"Look," I point at the lead male, a very chiseled, tan man with a mane of thick black hair like midnight silk. "See, he's very handsome."

Grandma squints at the TV. "Handsome," she repeats, although the man is no longer on the screen, having been replaced by a horse. To be fair, it is a very pretty horse.

"What's that you're reading?" I ask, seeing her beloved book again on her lap.

I've never seen Grandma do this, but she suddenly begins to bite her bottom lip—just like mom. For a fleeting moment, I panic that it's *Fifty Shades of Grey*, and I desperately tell myself that it hasn't been translated. But then she holds up her book for me to see, and I breathe a sigh of relief. *Biegły Pierwszy Krok - Z Polskiego Na Angielski* (Fluent First Step – Polish to English).

"You're learning English?"

Grandma looks as if she's trying to get the words out through a mouthful of rocks without dropping any of them, but slowly she says, "Yes. I am wanting to speak English."

"How come? Err," I correct my slang, "why?" Mom enrolled Grandma in English classes at REJC years ago and she hadn't had much of an interest then, saying she could get by just fine with only Polish. I wonder what changed, but Grandma won't answer, instead turning on me and asking why I'm not doing homework. I get the message—leave her alone, and she'll leave me alone.

Which brings me back to my phone and Noah's unanswered text.

I decide Mom's note will be easier to answer first.

While I'm waiting for the shower to warm up, I debate how best to tell mom I didn't go shopping today. I don't want to lie and say I actually went, and I also don't want to lie that I wasn't feeling well because Grandma will definitely sell me out, and Mom will have questions either way. So, after much deliberation, I scrawl a quick, vague reply.

Didn't shop today—had too much homework. Is Grandma learning English??

Oh man, if Grandma *is* learning English, I'm going to have to watch what I say in these notes. Not that I ever talk bad about Grandma in them, but I've been living with the understanding that they'd be for Mom's eyes only.

After a nice hot shower, I still don't have the words to reply to Noah, but I want to say something. So, as I'm getting dressed, I text him that's it's fine, all is forgiven, even though it's not. After he's been forgiven, Noah doesn't have much else to say. Why he was so desperate for me to talk to him, I don't understand. My gut tells me something is still amiss, but I don't have the energy for one more thing to be off kilter. There's enough going on as it is.

For once, I'm glad there's a grocery list pinned to the fridge. Mom didn't ask me to shop, but I need something to take my mind off the idea of Hannah and Madisen hanging out without me. I pull on my shoes and tie up my damp hair. "Grandma."

She doesn't respond. This time I think it has more to do with the *telenovela* still on TV than her not hearing me. She's sitting on the edge of the couch with her elbows on her knees.

"Grandma!"

"*Co?*"

"Do you want to go to the store with me?" I try first in English (what with her learning now) but when she doesn't respond, I switch to Polish. Grandma nods, and ten minutes later we're out the door—with Grandma's coupon-stuffed purse of course.

There are a few grocery stores in Fort Clemens, but the only one in walking distance is Market Fresh. It's downtown and only a tiny bit bigger than the coffee shop next door, but it has the essentials. It's brisk this morning, and a change of seasons is definitely in the air. My hair is still wet, and I didn't bring a jacket, so I try to usher Grandma along, but she's content at her waddle pace, and there is no getting her to hurry it up. By the time we make it, I'm starving and wondering why I asked Grandma to tag along in the first place.

I give her a few items to hunt for and take the rest for myself. The store is empty except for two cashiers up front and a lone stock boy wandering the aisles on his phone. He nearly bumps into me, but I step out of his way and don't get even a glance. I pivot like mad and try to see what's on his phone. Is it the video? He's about my age so it very well could be, but then again, I'm probably paranoid.

I'd thought a trip to the store would be relaxing, even therapeutic, but it seems that's not the case. As I'm searching for the right brand of rice, I hear the girls up front giggling, and my whole spine goes cold. How pathetic, they must think, out grocery shopping with her grandmother on a Saturday when everyone else is out with their friends. How much more pathetic it'll be next year when everyone is lounging around the dorms, going to sorority parties, and getting on with their lives while I'll still be right here, grocery shopping with my grandma.

There are only five of us in the small store, so I clearly hear it when one of the girls up front says, "I'm sorry? I don't understand what you're saying."

My blood runs cold, and I completely forget about the rice. I bolt out of the aisle only to see Grandma at one of the registers with her purse fanned out and her coupon bags laid out in front of the cashier. I freeze. Can I hide? Leave Grandma to get frustrated with the language barrier and hope she'll give up? No, she'll just come in search of me. So, with my fingers tingling and burning heat in my cheeks, I step up to Grandma's side and take possession of the coupons.

I can't look at her.

"She wants to use these coupons," I say, hardly above a whisper.

The cashier plucks one of the Ziplock bags up between two long, manicured fingers. I can feel the other girl staring at us, and my whole body locks up, as if that would make me invisible. "Okay, well these are good," our cashier says, separating three out of the bag, "but these other ones are expired."

I deeply consider not telling Grandma, but she'll know when she doesn't see the cashier scanning all the coupons.

So, with a heavy heart, I translate what the cashier said for Grandma.

"These good," she demands of the teenager across the desk. "These good." Two words in English aren't enough for Grandma to haggle the cashier into accepting, so she turns to me and asks me to.

I'm utterly embarrassed. We're arguing to save two dollars. These girls probably wouldn't bat an eye if they dropped two dollars in the street; it wouldn't be worth the effort to turn around and pick them up.

"Is there any way you can honor it?" My voice is getting quieter and quieter. "It's only a few days past." I finally meet the cashier's eyes, and I wish I hadn't. I recognize the cashier. MJ Booker—she's a junior in my history and calculus classes and a friend of Madisen's.

The corner of her lips raises as she recognizes me. "Oh, you're Katarina." She smiles, but it feels anything but friendly. "Of course. Anything for you."

Grandma is tugging on my sleeve, asking if we're going to get our savings, but I don't say anything. I feel like a lamb in a lion's den, and I don't yet know if they're going to let me walk out of here alive.

"$35.75" MJ says with another fanged smile. "I'm assuming that will be cash?"

I'm not sure how much money I give her, probably more than what I should, but I just want to get out. I scoop all the bags up myself and loop my arm through Grandma's to pull her out of the store. She's all of four feet five inches so she has to practically run to keep up with me. This time, when the girls are giggling as we're leaving the store, I know it's about me.

Grandma is pestering me to carry a bag, so I hand her the lightest of the bunch, hoping she'll leave me alone for the rest of the walk home. My head is spinning. Were they laughing at the coupons, or because it's me? Did they see the video? Well, that's a dumb question; of course MJ saw the video. I wish I'd said something, stood up for myself a little. Although, what would that have done but drawn me into a fight? MJ has always been a mean girl; even if she knows the accusation isn't true, she'll act like it is.

When we get home, I leave Grandma to put away the groceries and hide away in the bathroom. In the mirror, I notice right away that there's a pimple smack in the middle of my forehead. Maybe that's what the girls were laughing about, but probably not. It had to have been the video.

I sit on the edge of the tub, unlocking and relocking my phone. I want to tell someone about what happened, to be sure I'm not crazy and to have someone else say MJ and her friend are jerks, but who? I'm not sure I want to speak to Madisen *at all* ever again. Hannah is out with Madisen and she's weird about anything to do with the video. The girls on the team apparently are in the dark about this, and I want to keep it that way. Maybe Noah? But things are different between Noah and me now that I know he told Madisen about the day on the beach, and besides, he's Madisen's boyfriend. I can't really expect him to take my side.

I can feel the Post-it on the mirror staring at me. But no, I can't tell Mom either. For one thing, there's not enough Post-its left to write down all the things I'm feeling. And I can't just drop this on Mom. She'll worry, and the best thing I can do for her, better than grocery shopping, is not give her another reason to worry. I take a deep breath, lock my phone again, and tell myself to shake it off. This is just bullying; I can handle it.

Before I reenter the world, I add to my note to Mom. *Sorry I didn't get the rice.*

Chapter Ten

USUALLY DURING PRACTICE, MY mind wanders away. Sometimes I'm thinking about what homework I have for the night, other times I'm humming along to a song that's stuck in my head, but most of the time I'm dreaming of a huge Thanksgiving dinner because I'm *starving*. Today, however, I'm recounting all the ways that the day sucked, starting with this morning.

If I had any doubts that MJ saw Madisen's video, I didn't after first period. We are in the same history class, and MJ made a point of loudly whispering to anyone who would listen that I'd slept with Noah. For proof, she pointed them in the direction of Madisen's Instagram. I bolted out of class as soon as the bell rang as a small group was encircling my desk and throwing questions my way.

Lunch was equally great. After what happened at the swim meet, I wasn't sure if Hannah would even say hi to me, but she did, and she showed me a picture of the dress she'd picked out with the approval of Dina. In the picture, Hannah was wearing a floor-length, blush, A-line gown, and Madisen was standing beside her with her hands clamped onto Hannah's biceps. They were both beaming. It wasn't Hannah's intention, but seeing the picture made my stomach hurt, and I threw out the rest of my lunch. Which meant by the time I made it to calculus, my stomach was a rumbling machine.

Things weren't any better there. Madisen and I sit at the same cluster of desks, and it was deathly quiet between us—quiet enough to make our cluster-mates wonder what was up. That is, until MJ *happened* to share Madisen's Instagram post in our calculus group chat. While we were supposed to be working on a packet of problems, practically the whole class was watching Madisen's video. Suddenly I was public enemy number one to everyone except the three super smart kids at the front of the room.

If we had calculus before lunch, I would have texted back in the group chat that Madisen faked the video. But I was picturing Hannah wearing her bridesmaid dress with Madisen squeezing her tight, and it was hard to feel like Hannah wasn't already choosing Madisen over me. If I told everyone, it would certainly start something with Madisen again, and this time I might lose Hannah for good. Plus, would they really believe me? Isn't that what anyone would say to try and save face? It was better to not give the video any attention and hope that spoke volumes about its validity.

No one replied in the group chat, and no one said anything to me after class, but I could feel everyone's eyes on me when I stood up from my chair. It was enough to drive me to the decision that my friendship with Madisen was over. Even if she apologized, I wouldn't ever be her friend again. A friend doesn't do this, and a friend definitely doesn't sit back quietly and watch their friend burn.

So now, as I'm midway through a 300 freestyle drill, I push myself hard and imagine that with every stroke I'm putting distance between myself and Madisen.

"Does it feel warm in here to you?" Katie asks when we finish up the set.

The water does feel hot, but I thought it was just the fury inside me making it feel that way. "Yeah, a little."

In the lane over, Sean finishes up his set and comes up a panting mess. He chugs his entire water bottle in one gulp. Rachel is not-so-subtly watching him.

"Down girl," Kennedy whispers.

Rachel shakes her head and then escapes under the water only to pop up a second later. "Okay, yeah, it's really warm in here."

"Coach Kaitlin?" Katie waves her over. "We think something's wrong with the heater."

It turns out something is definitely wrong with the heater. The lifeguard checks the water twice, and it comes back at nearing ninety degrees, about ten degrees warmer than it ever should be. Practice isn't even halfway through, but the coaches have no choice but to cut it short. Normally, I'd love a day off, but today I was looking forward to turning off my brain in the water.

"Make sure you drink!" Coach Kaitlin shouts at all of us heading for the locker rooms.

"Water!" Coach Avery adds. "Not soda!"

Opening the door to the locker room is like opening the door to a freezer. "Oh, God, how hot was it in there?" I hear someone say. It feels like stepping out of a hot tub and straight into the snow. Everyone is racing to the showers to get warm. I hang back and out of their way, opting instead to just pull on my sweatpants and wait for the mad rush to die down. As I'm grabbing them out of my swim bag, I catch sight of the two twenty dollar bills I'd clipped to the inside pocket. I completely forgot!

"Rachel?" I don't see her anywhere around the lockers. Maybe she was lucky enough to get a shower. I have to squeeze through a clump of girls to get near the showers, and then it's almost impossible to hear with all the talking being amplified by the water. "Rachel?"

A blonde head pokes out of the spider shower. When she sees me she waves me over.

"No cutting!" someone yells.

"I'm not cutting!" I yell back into the mob of swimmers. "Geeze, this is nuts."

Rachel agrees. "Yeah, but seriously do you want this one next?"

"No, no. That group would kill me. I forgot to pay you for the shirts, though."

Rachel shakes her head, and a glob of conditioner hits my foot. "Oh, don't worry about it. Whenever."

"No, I've got it now, and I don't want to forget." I hand her the money, and she sticks it under her shampoo bottle. We're so different. Here I'd had that money laid flat in an envelope for college and then clipped into the inside of my bag so it'd stay safe, and Rachel puts it under her shampoo.

"They should be here this week," she says.

"Thanks for ordering them."

"Not a problem. You sure you don't want this shower? I'm almost done."

"It's all right. I don't mind waiting."

I don't mind waiting for all of ten minutes. The mob hasn't thinned much, and it seems like everyone is taking extra-long showers with practice getting out early. My hair is already pretty much dry, so I figure I'll just change here and shower at home. There are a few bathroom stalls in the locker room. I take my bag with me into one of those to get some privacy and elbow room. I strip out of my wet suit and let it hit the ground with a wet *plop*. As I'm rifling through my bag for my shoes, a bit of Sharpied graffiti catches my eye.

The first thing I notice is my name. It's bizarre to see my name written in handwriting other than my own or someone's I recognize, kind of like hearing my name called by a voice I don't know.

Katarina Dobek is a whore.

It could be comical because, first of all, I have never slept with anyone, so how on earth can I be a whore? But seeing this written here of all places makes my heart leap up into my throat. The video has penetrated the swim team.

I want to scrub my name off, except I realize, with a lump in my throat bringing tears to my eyes, people would just fill my name in even without it being on the wall.

I sit on the toilet and put my feet up on the seat so no one can see I'm in here. I'm not leaving until everyone is gone. What if whoever wrote this is out there, waiting for me to come out so they can see the look on my face after I've seen what they did? What if the whole team is hanging around in the locker room, waiting to accuse me of being a homewrecker?

Just as I'm thinking this, there's an eruption of high-pitched "Oooh's" and screaming. It makes me jump, and I pull my bag closer to my chest. Do they know I'm in here? Are they all watching the video together?

"Oh, my gosh!"

"You two are going to be such a cute couple!"

"Thanks!" I recognize this voice as Rachel's. She's over by the mirrors.

"Where is Sean taking you?"

"I don't know. I don't even know what day yet. He just asked if I want to go out sometime."

"*Awwww!*"

I want to go out there and fawn over Rachel and Sean's budding romance too, but I stay locked in my stall.

Because of the news, it takes longer than usual for the locker room to clear out. I count to thirty after I think I've heard the last person leave, and when I don't hear anyone else moving around, I crack the door to check if the coast is clear. The locker room is nothing but puddles and abandoned hair ties, so I throw my bag over my shoulder and slip out. I thought I'd made a clean escape, but I forgot to account for the one person who's always last out of practice—Nia.

She's sitting at one of the faded chairs in the hallway, going over what looks like next meet's roster, and her head lifts when I emerge. "Hey Kat. Running late? I thought everyone had left."

"Yeah… I was just…waiting on a shower."

Nia would have to be an idiot to believe that lie as my hair is bone dry and stiff with chlorine. She gives me a once over, and I know I'm caught. "Is something wrong?"

I shake my head. "No. I'm all right."

"If it's about the graffiti, I've already told Coach Avery about it. It'll be gone tomorrow."

I sink into the chair beside hers like a deflating balloon. "You saw?"

She nods. "I don't think a lot of people have."

"Do you know who did it?"

"In my experience," she says with a sad smile, "it won't change anything if I tell you."

"I've never seen anything written about you." Hearing things is another story.

"Well, that stall used to say *Nia Williams is a butch bitch*."

Those two words knock me back. I've heard them before, but it's so much worse knowing someone was out there calling Nia that. It's ludicrous and disgusting.

"I'm sorry," I say, not knowing what the right words are, if there are any.

Nia purses her lips for a second, then shakes her head. "I'm sorry, too. Sorry people like that exist, but they do. People can suck, but people like that don't matter, you know? It'll be all right, Kat."

"Thanks. I guess you saw the video too?"

Surprisingly, she shakes her head. "Someone sent it to me, but I deleted it. I don't have Instagram, and I don't care what goes on there. It's all fake anyway."

That brings a genuine smile out of me—one I didn't think I would be able to manage for a long time after today. "Thank you," I say again, truly meaning it.

"Nothing to thank me for. We've got a meet Saturday, don't forget."

"I won't," I say, picking up my bag. "See you there."

"See you, Kat."

As I'm walking home, I feel lighter than I have all day. Any time my thoughts drift to the video, I think of Nia and all she's endured and who she is today—captain of the swim team, respected, and an absolute powerhouse. Things will be okay; they were for Nia, and they will be for me.

Chapter Eleven

NIA'S PEP TALK SHIELDED me for all of a day. By Friday it isn't just graffiti in bathrooms anymore. People—people I don't even know—are texting me and coming up to me in the halls. Before morning practice starts, a brave sophomore with her hair up in a high ponytail ambushes me coming out of the locker room. "Hey you're Kat, right?"

Something about the way she asks tells me she definitely knows who I am.

"Yeah…"

"I was just wondering…well, what's up with you and Noah Hamilton?"

So it begins.

I roll my eyes and push past her, but I'm not immune to the sound of giggling behind my back. Maybe I should have denied anything happened between us. Is walking away just confirming what everyone already believes?

I jump into the water before the lane lines are put in and volunteer to swim them down the length of the pool just to get away from everyone for a minute. Most people will lazily swim breaststroke as they take the lane lines down, but I swim with my face in the water, hoping no one will see me and I can get through practice as invisible as possible. I hate this. I hate that Madisen has ruined everything, including swimming, just for stupid social media attention.

By the time I'm done getting the lane lines hooked in, everyone else is in the water, memorizing the set. It works out well for me because by the time I swim back, the first person in each lane has already started and there's no time to talk. I'm right behind Rachel, so as soon as I get to the wall, I push off to start our first set.

As I'm finishing up a 100 kick, someone tickles my toes. I *hate* it when people do that. I kick hard to try and get back on pace, but a second later that same person is touching my heel. I growl, and a smattering of bubbles blinds me. What is wrong with me? It feels like I'm going full speed, so why is this jerk on top of me?

We finish up the set, and I immediately whip around to see who the foot-toucher is. Isaac. He grins at me. "Tired today?" he teases.

Not in the mood, I ignore him and turn back to the whiteboard to see what's next—a 200 freestyle. That's perfect for me.

As I cut through the water, I push extra hard to put some space between Isaac and me. Maybe he's just having a great practice, but either way I don't want anyone touching my feet. The blue of the water starts to blur. The burn in my arms becomes familiar and constant and forgettable. I'm falling into my rhythm and so I let my mind wander. Instead of my usual homework daydreams, I find myself working out how exactly this became my senior year. I should be on top of the world, but instead I'm avoiding my teammates and spending more and more time on the couch. I didn't think life was going to be like this until after everyone went away to college.

Impossibly, I feel Isaac touch my big toe. In a moment of blind fury, I kick so hard that had his head been under my foot instead of his hand I would have knocked him out. My foot is throbbing, and I'm swimming significantly slower because of it, but Isaac lets up. Just like that, my rage is gone, and I'm incredibly embarrassed I did that. He didn't mean anything by it; he was just joking around, and now I might have broken his hand. How am I going to apologize to him when we're done with this set?

When we get to the end, I immediately turn and wait for Isaac to finish with guilt written all over my face. He stands, and even with his tinted goggles I can tell he's giving me a look like I'm a bomb about to go off. "I'm sorry," I say, loud enough for him to hear but low enough that it's private. "You can go in front of me."

Now he's looking at me like I've grown another head. Maybe I have, because old Kat *never* would have given up her superior spot. Especially to one of the twins.

I spend the rest of practice chasing Isaac's bubbles. Sometimes I'm so far behind him that I can't even see his feet. With Sam out sick today, there's no one behind me, and somehow, after every set, I'm the last one finished out of the whole team. Eventually, I just keep my face in the water as I glide in, hoping to go unnoticed, like trash in the ocean floating by as everyone else times their start for the next set.

I can't hide out in the locker room while everyone else gets changed this time because class starts in twenty minutes. My plan instead is to change as quickly as possible and read in my first period classroom until the bell rings. I change in record time, not stopping to see if the graffiti has been removed like Nia said. I have one foot out the door when I hear someone call my name. My whole body tenses.

"Kat, wait up!"

I exhale a sigh of relief. It's just Rachel.

I pivot and do my best to genuinely smile. "Hey Rachel. Congrats on the date with Sean."

"Oh, thanks! I guess you were right about him liking me. But here, I wanted to give you your shirt before I forget." She digs in her bag and pulls out a scarlet spirit jersey with "FREESTYLE" across the back in chunky white letters.

"Wow. These turned out awesome!" I hold the shirt up to my torso, making sure it'll fit. "Thanks for getting these."

"No problem! We're the best relay team, so we should look the part."

I feel good after that, like maybe the whole school doesn't hate me or have this awful perception of me. I mean, here are three girls that want me on their team, that are part of a group and want to include me in it. I'm practically walking on air. Until first period starts. When MJ walks in, I feel the worry start to creep back in. What if Rachel, Katie, and Kennedy are just slow to get the news in Franklin High School? What happens when they see the video or hear about it? Are they still going to want me to be a part of the team? I find myself checking my backpack more than once to make sure my shirt is still there, that it hasn't been revoked.

When lunch rolls around, I stand in front of the cafeteria doors without the willpower to go through them. Hannah and I still sit together, but we're not friends the way we used to be, and I feel it every time I'm around her. Plus, I don't trust myself not to say something I'll regret if she brings up anything about Madisen, like the bridesmaid dress shopping.

The halls clear out, and I can hear the noise level steadily rising in the cafeteria as people get settled. I feel silly standing in front of the doors. I need to make a decision. Will Hannah be upset if I'm not there? Maybe... I mean, no one likes to sit by themselves at lunch. But then again, she wasn't upset when I wasn't there dress shopping or at Madisen's

Halloween party (the one I learned about through Instagram).

I turn around and head for the library instead.

Students at Franklin High School are allowed to spend their lunch hour in the library working on homework or getting extra help with subjects they're struggling in. Very few people actually do. Most just bring their homework to lunch and copy their friends' answers, so when I enter the library it's as quiet as church. There's only one other kid sitting at the desks set up for lunch studiers, and he has headphones on and a stack of ACT prep books beside him.

I choose one of the desks in the back by the windows and take out *The Scarlet Letter* along with my lunch so I look busy. I don't bother even opening the book to where we left off; I'm too busy staring at my phone and wondering when/if Hannah will text me wondering where I am.

The text comes after I've finished my sandwich.

Are you coming to lunch?

No, I text back, *I had some homework I wanted to work on.*

It's not really a lie, but Hannah and I both know that if I wanted to get homework done, I could've done it at our lunch table. She doesn't text me back, and I feel a little guilty about ditching her, but not as bad as I would have felt sitting in awkward silence with her.

I spend the rest of my lunch trying to relax in the sanctuary of the library because my next class is the one I've been dreading the most—calculus. After MJ shared the video in our class group chat, real or imagined, it seems like everyone is ping-ponging their eyes between Madisen and me. I think they're waiting for one of us to explode.

I take my seat at our desk cluster and immediately train my eyes on the board where they will remain the rest of class. Madisen comes in not a minute later. I can feel her pull her chair out and set her book on the desk. I can feel someone's eyes on me, but really it could be anyone in class.

As soon as the bell rings, Ms. Khan stands and begins writing on the board. She's wearing a black and white polka dot skirt and a black T-shirt that says, "Sorry I'm late, I took the rhombus." Noah doesn't take calculus, so I file that one away to tell him later.

"All right, class," Ms. Khan says with all the excitement of a mega math nerd, "we're going to continue with proofs today."

There's a general groan of dread from the class. I don't hate proofs, but what does sink my stomach is seeing Madisen pull out her phone in my peripheral vision.

"We're going to prove the chain rule. Does anyone remember what the chain rule tells us?"

Is she texting or posting? Replying to comments? Is something going on in our class group chat again? I inch my phone out of my pocket and steal a glance, but I don't have any new notifications.

"Katarina?"

"Um…" I swallow hard. Why did she have to call on me? If I get the answer right, half the class will find a reason to hate me for that, and if I get it wrong, the other half will go around calling me stupid. I try to convey my crisis through my eyes to Ms. Khan. Either she reads me loud and clear or she's too excited to keep waiting. "MJ?"

"How to find the derivative."

"Of a composite function," Ms. Khan adds.

I get lucky; this ends up being one of the classes where Ms. Khan uses up the entire period teaching and we don't have any work time. There's no time for whispers or texts or for anyone to see whatever Madisen was doing on her phone. I book it out of the room as soon as the bell rings and bask in the small victory of having made it through another class with Madisen and MJ.

I'm in a much better mood at afternoon practice than I was this morning. I circle up to stretch with my lane instead of putting in the lane lines and even laugh when Isaac teases that I broke his hand earlier (Rachel high fives me). I'm in such a good mood that I don't go out of my way to avoid Noah. And sure enough, as I'm leaving school, I bump right into him.

"Sorry I'm late," I say as I fall in step with him, "I took the *rhombus*."

Noah doesn't laugh. He doesn't even smile.

"Hey," all humor is gone from my voice, "what's wrong?"

"Nothing."

"I don't buy that. Did something happen at practice?"

"No."

"Is it a family thing?"

"No."

"Do you not want to talk about it?"

Noah sighs, and I notice the corner of his eye looks a bit shiny . He's been crying. I bite my lip as all the worst scenarios come to mind.

"Madisen and I broke up."

Admittedly, that wasn't one of the things that came to mind as a *worst scenario*.

"Mutually?" I ask, although it seems like a dumb question seeing as Noah has been crying.

"More or less. It wasn't right."

I place my hand on his shoulder and my spine tingles. I think this is the first time I've actually touched Noah since he and Madisen started dating. It's awful, I definitely shouldn't think it, but I wonder if he felt it too.

"Are you okay?" It's the generic thing to say to someone after any range of tragedy, but seeing as I've never exactly been team *Nadisen*, I don't know what else to say. I'm not mourning the relationship death, but jumping for joy isn't appropriate either.

"Yeah, I'm fine. Listen," Noah turns and really looks at me. "I'm sorry for everything that's happened. I'm sorry Madisen made that video and posted it. I know you've been getting shit for it, and it's not right."

"You mean you're not also getting called a whore?" I tease, trying to lighten the air between us.

Noah winces. "You're not a whore."

"I know."

He rubs the back of his neck, and I take note of the line of his bicep. I feel greedy, letting my heart suddenly feel all these butterflies and staring at every handsome inch of Noah from his head to his toes, but I'm finally allowed to. Noah is single. Is it so bad to fall back into dreams of us being together?

"I'm so sorry. You shouldn't have to deal with this. I wish I would've seen Madisen's true colors a lot sooner."

I inhale, but there's no exhale to follow. Am I dreaming? Am I reading too much in between the lines? Could Noah actually have broken up with Madisen because of the video and all the damage it's done to me? My heart sings. It makes sense! Noah was a victim of bullying; he wouldn't want anything to do with someone who could do something like that.

It takes everything in me to get control of my voice and not explode in giddy giggles. "Me too."

"Is it really bad?" Noah asks.

"What?" I'm brought back to earth. "What people are saying?"

"Yeah. How bad is it?"

I think about all the people that have come up to me (the sophomore on the swim team, MJ, Allison Murphy in gym class) and then the graffiti and the calculus group chat. Not to mention the hundreds of comments on Instagram that I refuse to look at. "It's not great," I admit.

"Can you get the video taken down?"

I shake my head. "Madisen won't do it; she's getting too many followers from it."

"What about Instagram? Can you report it?"

I shrug. "I've thought about it, but it's not clearly bullying. You'd have to see all the off-camera stuff that happened after to understand."

"What about that then?"

"What about what?"

"What about what happened after the video? Can you do something with that?"

"How? Madisen didn't record that, and even if she did there's no way she would give it to me."

He shakes his head. "No, I mean like make a statement or something. You could post something on Instagram to say everything that happened."

Use my Instagram for something other than swim team pictures? "I don't know…"

"Why not?"

"Because…well, shouldn't I not be shedding more light on it? Wouldn't posting something like that just make this a bigger deal?"

"But isn't it already a big deal?"

He has a point. The story of Madisen accusing me of sleeping with Noah has infiltrated the entire school, including the swim team. What's the risk then? That more people will think worse of me? Maybe not. Maybe more people will be like Noah; I mean, Noah broke up with Madisen because of this, because of me. He's here for me, so maybe more people will be too; maybe even Hannah. The people that care about me will be there for me once they know the truth.

Chapter Twelve

I BREATHE OUT SLOWLY to steady my heart. If I do this, I'm officially ending my friendship with Madisen. There is no going back. *When* I do this, class is going to be more awkward, there will be more gossip, and Hannah is going to find herself smack in the middle. But how can I not? I steel myself knowing whoever cares about me will be there when the dust settles. I'd rather know than trust fake smiles.

I can count on my hand the number of times I've planned a social media post and really, that's being generous because I'm counting birthdays and Christmases where I made sure I did my hair and stood in a specific spot for the photo. Otherwise, this will be the first Instagram post I've sat down and planned, even taken notes on. I wonder if this is what Madisen does every time. I feel incredibly silly doing it, even though I'm alone in my room.

Mom is at the hospital, and Grandma is practicing more with her book. Now that the secret is out, she's not shy about practicing her pronunciations. She must be in the food lesson because she's been saying "potato" to herself for the last twenty minutes. I'd really love to be helping her because this would be the most fun English lesson to teach (i.e. going through our pantry and fridge and swapping our Polish and English names for everything), but I want to do this before I lose my nerve.

I prop my phone against some books on my dresser and sit sideways on my bed so in the camera I look sort of like I'm hosting a talk show in my bedroom. It's not exactly what I'm going for, but it lets me discretely hide my notes on the floor.

On my first attempt, I look right into the camera and instantly freeze up. It's really weird to be talking to my phone, especially when I see myself being recorded on the screen. I shuffle across the floor, delete that one, and try again.

"My name is Katrina—"

I groan and get up to stop the recording. Messing up my own name! Seriously? This is entirely stupid. I don't know why I'm stressed out about trying to make this video perfect when really all I want to do is hold my phone at arm's length and say, "Madisen Grace is a big fat liar. Exhibit A…" and be on my merry way. But if I'm going to tell my side, the *truth*, I have to keep my composure. I can't get upset or people will think I'm only doing this for attention and won't hear a word I'm saying.

Before I press record for the third time, I shake out my hands and feet to try and loosen my nerves. When I sit back down on my bed, I take another settling breath. This time, I train my eyes just above my phone, and I'm finally able to speak. "My name is Katarina Dobek, and everything you've heard about me is a lie. I'm not a whore, and I'm not a homewrecker either. Two months ago, my former friend, Madisen Grace, posted a video accusing me of sleeping with her boyfriend." I choose to keep Noah's name out of it. This is not about him.

"For the record, I have never slept with him…or anyone. Not that it's anyone's business, but apparently now it is." I take a deep breath to steady the boiling anger I can feel creeping up from my stomach. "Madisen stopped recording before she told me that her accusation was a joke and she would be posting it for content to get more followers on Instagram. I asked her not to, and she did anyway. The video is a lie. Madisen has already admitted it to me and one other person." I also don't say Hannah's name. This is between Madisen and me.

"I asked Madisen to take the video down because people have been harassing me, and she refused. In fact, she told me to *get over it*. I'm not over it. Clearly Madisen no longer wants to be my friend, and that's fine. But I will not let her keep dragging my name through the mud. I'm not a whore. I haven't done anything to Madisen. So instead of harassing me, and writing about me on bathroom walls," I add, shooting a pointed stare at the camera, "ask Madisen to tell the truth or just leave it all alone."

When I stop the recording, my hands are buzzing with adrenaline, and I feel simultaneously like I can move mountains and like I can't breathe. I watch the video back and it pumps me full of anxiety. Somehow, I can't win. Seeing this from Madisen's perspective, I know I'll be starting World War III, because how *dare* I call her a liar. But nevertheless, I edit out me walking to and from my bed and post the video to Instagram before I talk myself out of it. It's me. It's raw, it's pure, and it's true. If Madisen's upset, well, I just don't care anymore.

The temptation to sit on Instagram and see how many people have watched my video is strong, but I hear Grandma working her way to correctly saying "vinegar," so I leave my phone in my room and help her instead.

• • •

Unfortunately, Grandma only had about an hour of studying left in her before she headed to bed. We made it through all the fruits and vegetables we had in the house but got sidetracked arguing whether *Rosół* would be "chicken soup" or "*Rosół*" in English. Grandma did not like me simplifying her recipe to *just* chicken soup, and I'm not sure she entirely forgave me before going to bed.

Today is a rare Friday night during swim season where there isn't a meet the next morning, so I don't want to waste it with homework. However, this is also my first free Friday night when I don't have any friends. I could call Noah, but given the video I just posted it feels a little too soon. Hannah would probably small talk with me, but after ditching her at lunch and given how's it been between us, I doubt she'd want to hang out. The swim girls are an option, but I'm sure they've already secured their plans. Rachel might actually be on her date with Sean right now.

Is this what next year will be like? Am I going to spend every weekend trying to find someone who's still in Fort Clemens to hang out with? Swimming will be over, my friends will be gone—if I have any left by the end of the year —and I'll have just a class or two a day at the community college. What do people do all day? How do they fill up all the nothingness between scattered obligations? For right now, my answer is Instagram.

As I get my phone, there's a logical part of my brain (maybe my inner defense system) telling me to turn it off and not look at it for a long time. I know what I'm going to see, so why subject myself to it?

Because I'm bored. I'm bored and the temptation really is too great. What if my video is flooded with comments of support? How wonderful will it feel to see so many people believe me. Monday could actually be a normal day where all this Instagram nonsense gets left in the past.

But as I open the app, I realize that won't happen this Monday.

Seventy-two notifications. I have never had any app on my phone, even my neglected email, with seventy-two notifications. As I make my way over to my video, the number keeps growing.

There are very few likes in respect to how many comments there are. I know what that means, and my heart starts to race. I should turn back now while I can.

It's not too late.

I definitely shouldn't read any of them.

Definitely shouldn't scroll down.

Yeah, okay, fake bitch.

First you sleep with her boyfriend, then you go gaslighting her on Insta? What's your problem?

Smells a little convenient to me.

My eyes are burning, either from not blinking as I keep scrolling through the comments or from tears at reading them. It was all for nothing then. Madisen's 70,000 followers are judge, jury, and executioner, and I am beyond a doubt guilty in their eyes. I can't pull myself away. I keep refreshing my profile to see if the newest comment is in my favor. There has to be at least one person who believes me.

My eyes rake through the comments for usernames I know. Has Hannah seen it? She knows it was all a lie just as well as I do. I think for a moment about texting her, asking her if she's seen my post and if she'll speak up, but I don't. I chose not to say her name to keep her out of it, like she asked; I can't then ask her to get involved. She may not be being fair to me, but that doesn't mean I'm not going to be fair to her. I look for Noah's username too. Where is he? Wasn't he the one that encouraged me to do this? Surely he will comment and say it's true, nothing happened between us.

The notifications slow. As the hour creeps closer to six in the morning, they stop altogether. Everyone is asleep. This is my momentary reprieve before it all begins again in a few hours. I scan through one more time for Noah. Nope. Nowhere. Maybe he hasn't seen it yet, but still my stomach twists not seeing even *him* support me.

My back is sore from sitting in one place for so long. I stand and stretch and scold myself for not getting to bed earlier. But as I'm getting ready to do so, I hear a car pull up outside. Mom's home.

I freeze. If Mom sees me up, she'll know something is wrong. But as soon as I hear the engine shut off, all I can think about is getting wrapped up in a tight hug, and my feet are glued to the floor.

Mom pushes the door open slowly, tiptoeing into the house, not noticing me right away. Strands of her hair have fallen out of her ponytail, her powder blue scrubs are wrinkled, and there are dark circles under her eyes. Yet, when she sees me standing in the hall, she breaks into a wide grin. "What are you doing up?" she whispers.

I step forward to hug her, but Mom holds her hands up. "Let me change out of my scrubs." Her smile drops, and I can feel her looking me over. "Is everything okay?"

"Yeah," I lie, holding back tears, "just couldn't sleep."

I don't think Mom believes me, but she lets it lie for the moment so she can go change. I sink back down on the couch and wipe at my eyes. The bursting dam feeling is going away, and I feel stupid for almost losing it in front of Mom. So what if people are being mean on the internet? I should never have read any of the comments, and I vow not to from here on.

Mom tiptoes back, now dressed in an old T-shirt and sweatpants, and holds her arms out for a hug. I happily let myself be swallowed up by her embrace. I can smell her shampoo, and it and the beat of her heart against mine washes away any worry. "Everything okay?" she whispers against my temple, leaving a kiss there too.

I pull back and nod. "Everything's fine. How was work?"

"Good! We delivered a set of twins."

"Boys? Girls? One of each?"

"Two boys," Mom says, smiling at the memory. "Charlie and Jack."

"That's awesome. You're pretty awesome, Mom."

Mom wraps her arm around my shoulders and squeezes me close. "That's because I have an awesome daughter. Are you going back to bed or are you up now?"

I don't tell Mom that I haven't actually gone to sleep at all tonight/this morning. "What are you doing?"

"I'm not tired just yet. Want to catch up on Hollywood Housewives?"

I also don't tell Mom that I've seen every episode at least twice. I'd re-watch anything to spend time with her.

Mom sits in the middle of the couch, and I curl up next to her, resting my head on her shoulder. We have the TV on mute with closed captions so we don't wake Grandma (although she's probably already waking up). Mom is stroking my hair, and it's lulling me into a dream-like state. She says something, and it takes a minute for the words to crawl from my ears to my brain. "Grandma said you've been home a lot more."

"Senior year is a lot harder than I thought it would be," I say with my heart like a stone in the pit of my stomach.

"Lots of homework?"

"Yeah."

"How are your friends?"

I swallow thickly. "It's different for them."

Mom's hand moves to my scalp, and she rubs little circles with her fingers. "I'm sorry we can't afford a four-year anniversary."

I feel awful. That's not what I meant at all, and now Mom thinks it's her fault. "It's not that," I hurriedly say. "They have different classes."

Mom bites her lip. "I wish I could give you more."

I sit up and turn so that Mom and I are face to face. I take her hands and tell her the truth. "You've given me *everything*."

Mom smiles sadly and pulls me into another hug. I squeeze her tight, hoping she knows I mean it. There are not enough words to say thank you for everything she's done. Mom gave me a life steps ahead of her own, just as Grandma did for her. There's no way to say thank you for that in any language.

I don't remember falling asleep, but when I wake up my head is on Mom's lap, and Mom is sound asleep. As I blink awake, I carefully disentangle myself and slink away to the kitchen. Grandma is there, drinking a cup of tea and reading her book. She glances up and smiles at me. "Good morning, Katarina," she says in perfect English.

Chapter Thirteen

BECAUSE MOM AND I fell asleep on the couch and Mom is subsequently still there, I take my cup of coffee outside. We're entering November, and the days of shorts and sandals are definitely over. Despite the sunshine, it's brisk, and my cardigan is not going to cut it for very long. I move my lawn chair into the sun to soak up as much of warmth as I can.

My phone is nearly dead, and there are over one hundred notifications in my Instagram app. I'm tempting fate by looking at any of them, but I have to know if Noah commented. So, preparing for the slaughter, I go to my profile. I purposefully scroll at a pace too fast to read anything more than the username of the commenter, and even then, I don't read the whole name. I'm looking for an *N,* and if the username doesn't start with that, then I quickly fly past it to the next. That's how I make the mistake of reading a comment by *norahawthorn.*

This is so fake. Watch @madisen_grace's livestream for the truth.

It is probably the worst thing I could have read as I'm emotionally compromised. I imagine this is what it would feel like to literally be stabbed in the back. Noah was the one that put this idea in my head; *he* was the one who asked how bad it has been. Well, a lot worse now that he hasn't taken the time to stand in solidarity with me!

Did you see my post? Why didn't you comment? I text him with shaking fingers.

I wait exactly two minutes (I'm watching like a hawk for his reply) before he says. *Sorry, sorry. I'll go now.*

It hardly pacifies me. Why did I do this? Why didn't *Noah* make a video calling Madisen out? He's just as much involved, and he knows just as well as I do that it's not true. Is it because it's not as bad for him…because he's a guy? It doesn't seem fair that getting the truth out rests entirely on my shoulders.

And Madisen replied? I'm already on Instagram waiting for Noah to comment, so it's all too easy to hop over to Madisen's profile and see what her livestream was all about.

Surprisingly, she hasn't blocked me on Instagram. Naively, I think maybe that means she's a little sorry and feels bad about ending our friendship. But as soon as I start watching the posted livestream, I realize it's not that at all.

The first thing I think is that this is the first time I've seen Madisen without makeup on. She has definitely outdone me when it comes to *raw*. Her face is red and blotchy from acne and irritation usually concealed under a layer of concealer. Her eyes are still alarmingly blue, but there are puffy half-moons under them and a crease down her forehead deep enough to lose a penny in. A wreck would be the perfect way to describe her. This is not Madisen like I've known her.

She sniffles and for the first minute or so says nothing. I'm just watching her hold back tears and snot. It's not pretty. But then, as she starts speaking, I understand. Madisen wants me to see this. *She's doing this on purpose.*

"Hi, everyone," she wipes at her baggy, but dry, eyes, "I'm sorry I don't really look like me or…sound like me." Her eyes start to well up, and it's like watching the tide coming in, about to smash me and my rinky-dink boat against the rocks. "It's been an *awful* day." *WHAM!* Here come the tears, and there goes my boat in a spray of saltwater and splinters. Big, fat crocodile tears roll down her cheeks, and a smattering of heart emojis flood the comments from the other people watching.

It's okay, Mads!
We love you!

I'm glued to my phone although my gut is telling me to shut it down and run.

"So," pause for a long, rattling sigh, "Noah b-broke up with me."

Oh no.

More hearts flood the comments.

"I don't want to get into it, but…"

The *but* comes right as someone in the comments says what I'm thinking and what I'm sure everyone else is thinking. "For Katarina?"

Madisen doesn't confirm, but she might as well. "…he left me for someone else. It's all my f-fault. I knew there was something going on. My head knew they were too close to be just friends, but my h-heart didn't want to believe it. E-even when he told me that she made a…a move on him I didn't want to believe it. And I was stupid. *So stupid.*"

You're NOT stupid, Madisen!
Karma is coming for them!
Cheaters get what they deserve!

"I thought she was my friend. I thought he loved me." A big fat tear rolls down her cheek, and her lower lip quivers.

"I'm going to be taking a b-break from social media for a little bit. I love you all very much."

I close out of the live stream in shock. I'm about to turn my phone off completely, but a last notification comes in. This has to be Noah's comment, so I click on it.

Katarina is telling the truth. Nothing happened between us and nothing ever will--——

"God, Noah!" I bang my coffee cup on the arm of the chair, and lukewarm coffee spills all over me. I can't breathe. Everything is crumbling. And then to get kicked like that!

Thank God I thought to go outside because the tears come in full force and quickly turn to sobs. It's over—all of it. Madisen won, and anything she says about me from now on is gospel, and Noah...

He said it perfectly himself: nothing happened between us and nothing ever will.

Chapter Fourteen

I'M SICK MONDAY; NOT with anything Grandma or Mom can diagnose, but nevertheless unable to get out of bed. Every time I think about going to school, seeing my classmates, seeing *Madisen*, my stomach cramps. I spend the day on the couch watching daytime TV with Grandma, wondering if I have enough credit hours to graduate early and never have to go back. As far as I see it, there's nothing left for me at Franklin High School.

Or so I think, until I get Nia's text at dinner.

Were you at school today? You missed both practices.

I completely forgot.

No, I'm sorry. I was out sick today. I forgot to tell Coach Avery. Will you be here tomorrow?

You have to love that about Nia; she's frank and to the point, no fluff. She brings up a good question, though. Is there a way I can be at practice but not at school? But even the idea of going to practice fills me with dread. Surely the bathroom graffiti artist will have seen Madisen's livestream along with whoever else has been following the drama. For all I know, the whole team is laughing at me behind my back.

But this is also my last year of swim. There are only a few more meets, and I want to soak up every minute of them while I still can. Not only that, but even if they hate me, I can't leave Rachel, Kennedy, and Katie to be disqualified because I'm not there to swim. That wouldn't be fair to them to end their senior season on the bench.

Yeah, I'll be there.

Good. Meet Saturday. Don't forget.

I'll be there.

· · ·

I'm shaking, and it has nothing to do with the cold water. I heard my name clear as a bell in the locker room. Subtlety has gone out the window. I am public enemy number one.

Rachel dives in and surfaces just a foot away from me. "Feeling better?" she asks.

"Not really." I didn't eat breakfast this morning for fear it would all come right back up.

She nods her head to the lane where a group of juniors are loudly talking about me. "Don't worry about them. They don't know anything."

"...she slept with Noah Hamilton! The football player."

I sink a little lower in the water. "Thanks, but it's kind of hard not to."

"They're stupid. Those are the same girls that last year said I had eleven toes. One of them even asked to see it. They're not the sharpest crayons in the box."

Well, at least one person doesn't hate me.

"Thanks, Rachel."

"Don't worry about it. I also told my cousins to shut up about it."

I know she said it to make me feel better, but now I'm worrying Sam and Isaac also think it's true. I don't meet their eyes when they get in the lane, and I stick close to Rachel all practice to have someone to appear busy talking with. I'm pretty sure she figures out that I'm using her as a human shield because she waits for me to shower, waits for me to finish getting changed in the locker room, and walks with me to my first period class.

"Thank you—"

"Nothing to thank me for," she says with a wink. "You're saving me from having to wait for Sean. That boy is *always* late, and it gives me anxiety."

Unfortunately, Rachel's first class is across the school, so I'm alone in my history class when MJ comes in. She's like a heat-seeking missile, never slowing and coming right for me. We're the only two in the classroom, and she pulls up a chair in the desk next to mine. I pretend not to notice, all the while thinking I should've waited for school to start in a bathroom stall.

I can feel her eyes boring into my skull, and I picture that better-than-you smirk on her face—the same one she had on at Market Fresh.

"Do you have something to say?" I ask through gritted teeth.

"Oh, no. No. Just watching."

I shake my head, knowing I shouldn't bother with her. But still I say, "Watching what? I'm sure there are lots of things more interesting than the side of my head."

"Yes, I'd rather look at anything other than your rat's nest of hair." My cheeks burn, and I bite the inside of my cheek. "But I've just started dating Eli McKinney, and I want to make sure you don't decide to come after him next."

It takes everything in me to keep my head facing forward and not to give her the satisfaction of being able to read my face. "You know as well as everyone else that Madisen lied about everything."

"Do I?" I can hear the smirk in her voice.

Blessedly, the bell rings, and more students file in. MJ scoops up her things, but doesn't leave without bending close and saying, "It doesn't matter."

It's not what she said that makes me want to sink through the floor and disappear, it's knowing that she's right. I don't hear a word our teacher says all class, and when our tests are passed out, I'm in a daze. Are the words on the paper in English? I read the same question over and over, unable to make any sense of it. I spend so much time on that question that when there are only five minutes of class left, I haven't made it past the first page. Panic races up my spine. I'm going to fail. As soon as I realize that, my brain completely locks up, and I'm sitting in a stupor until the bell rings.

My day doesn't improve.

I hear my name in the halls at least five times a passing period, and never are the people talking *to* me. Allison Murphy calls me a whore in gym class, and apparently I didn't lock my locker all the way because someone puts the lock on backwards so I have to get on my knees to undo it. Even the librarian, Ms. Summers, looks at me differently when I come to hide out during lunch. It wouldn't surprise me if she's also seen Madisen's videos.

My stomach aches when it comes time for calculus, and I debate going to the nurse and begging to be released for the day. I just want to go home. But going home means no afternoon practice, and if I miss again, I could get pulled from the meet. Plus I still have a friend in Rachel, and I don't want to lose her too.

Madisen is already seated and looks the polar opposite of how she did in her Instagram livestream. Her hair is blown out, and her eyes are alight. There's no sign of the sniveling mess from a few nights ago. It makes me all the more nervous to sit near her.

MJ comes in and passes by our desk cluster. She stops at Madisen's desk and puts a hand on her shoulder. "So sorry to hear about you and Noah," she says, loud enough for everyone else to hear. "He didn't deserve you, and they'll get what they deserve." Her words are so venomous that even the super smart kids in the front of the class turn to see who she's glaring at.

Ms. Khan bursts into the room like a tumbleweed of paper and Expo markers. "All right, all right," she says. "I know the bell hasn't rung yet, but it's our last day to review proofs before the exam, and I don't want you to miss a moment. Madisen, will you pass these out for me?"

Madisen hops up and takes a stack of review packets from Ms. Khan's desk. Our desk cluster is in the middle of the room, and it seems she's making every effort to make it her last stop. When she does come to our desks, she places a packet on Eric's and Violet's desks, one on hers, and then looks at me pointedly before taking the rest back to Ms. Khan's desk. Eric and Violet are just coming in, so they don't notice the gleam in her eyes when she sits back down.

Without a word, I stand to go get my own. "Need something, Katarina?" Ms. Khan asks as she writes busily on the white board.

I pick up one of the packets. "I didn't get one," I say and return to my seat.

Something is wrong though. Something about my desk feels different than the way I left it. Madisen is looking at the board, but she's smiling, so I scan my things as nonchalantly as I can. My backpack is still there, so are my books, and my pencil is still in its place.

My blood runs cold. Where is my phone? I brush my hand over my pocket, but it's not there, and I distinctly remember placing it on top of my desk.

"All right, you should all have a review packet on your desk," Ms. Khan says.

"Where is my phone?" I whisper across the desks at Madisen.

She pretends she doesn't hear me and starts working on the first problem in our packet.

"Madisen," I say more firmly, "where is my phone?"

"How should I know?" she bites back without lifting her head.

"Because you took it."

"Why would I take your phone?"

I can feel Violet's eyes ping-ponging between us. "Because you have some kind of problem with me."

She snorts and goes back to her packet.

The boys in middle school used to do this kind of thing to Noah where they would hide his gym uniform or his backpack. He told me once that even though it bothered him, he'd always act like it didn't, like he didn't care if he never saw that object again, and then the bullies would eventually get tired of the game and his things would show up.

I try to channel that same energy and focus on our review packet, but I'm having trouble doing basic addition because all I can think is *where is my phone?* I think about raising my hand and telling Ms. Khan my phone has gone missing, but that will only get me in trouble for having my phone out in class, and Madisen will keep it so she doesn't get in trouble too.

"Madisen, just give me my phone back."

She ignores me, and my stomach starts to churn. No, that's not it. It's anger boiling in there. My cheeks grow hot, and my fingers get jittery with impatience and pent-up frustration.

"All this for Instagram followers? Really? You are pathetic." As the words leave my lips, I don't regret them at all. In fact, I wish I'd said them months ago.

Now Madisen hears me. She puts down her pencil and glares at me. "Pathetic is stealing another girl's boyfriend because you can't get your own."

Eric's eyes are also playing table tennis now.

"Don't forget to show your work!" Ms. Khan singsongs. "Without proof it doesn't count."

Without proof it doesn't count.

"Where's *your* proof, Madisen? Why don't you drop the act already? You know nothing happened with me and Noah. You made it all up so you could get more free yoga pants and water bottles and stupid shit. And you know what, Madisen? Noah broke up with you because he saw it too. You're so damn fake now you're not even a person."

I didn't realize my voice was steadily rising, but suddenly the rest of the class is dead silent.

Madisen slowly rises from her seat. "Seventy thousand people believe me," she says, every word dripping with malice. "How many believe you?"

I stand as well and look her dead in the eyes. These eyes used to belong to my best friend, someone I trusted and cared for, and now all I see is hate reflected back at me. "Not a single *fucking* one."

"Ms. Dobek!" Ms. Khan shouts, voice reaching a hysteric octave. I realize Madisen and I must look like two lionesses getting ready to tear each other's throat out. "Detention! Now!"

Ms. Khan has never once given a detention, and I'm sure, in my cooled-down logical brain, she's just panicking at having the beginnings of a fight in her classroom. But the unjustness of shouldering the blame, after I've been carrying the weight of Madisen's victimization for months, pushes me over the edge. I throw my bag over my shoulders and plant myself between Madisen and MJ's desk. MJ, for her part, looks like a deer caught in headlights. "Whichever of you has my phone, give it back. *Now*."

Madisen glares. MJ, however, reveals my phone under her notebook and hands it to me with wide eyes. I rip it out of her hand and begrudgingly take the pink detention slip Ms. Khan is holding out to me.

Chapter Fifteen

DETENTION WOULD NOT BE so bad if I weren't
missing practice for it. Apparently (this is my first time going),
they hold detention in the study hall room. The classroom is
long and narrow and completely empty except for desks
arranged in four rows. There are two kids already here: a guy
wearing a red hoodie who is asleep on his desk in the back,
and MJ. Seeing her here makes me feel a little less sour; at
least she got in trouble for provoking me.

I hand my detention slip to the teacher on duty, Mrs.
Foresta, our Spanish teacher. Her hair is wisps of sandy curls,
and she has the demeaner of an old bulldog. For a woman
who's fluent in two languages, she's rather nonverbal and
simply grunts to acknowledge my attendance.

Not that I think she would try to talk to me, but I
choose a desk as far away from MJ as I can get. She doesn't
lift her head as I cross the room.

The rules of detention are written on the board in
marker and look like they've been there for years.

No talking.

No phones.
No music.
No sleeping.
One bathroom break.

Seeing as the boy in the hoodie is drooling and snoring, it doesn't seem like Mrs. Foresta is much of a rule enforcer. She herself is reading a June edition of *People* magazine with a photo of Jude Law on the cover: *Baby Number 6!*

I have plenty of homework and a calculus test to study for, but I don't feel like doing any of it. Instead, I sneak my phone out and send a quick text to Nia. Hopefully she's not in the water yet.

Hey Nia, I'm not going to be at practice. I'm sorry.

It's 2:50 now. Practice probably already started. Shit. Nia is going to be livid. I rack my brain for how many practices we're allowed to miss before we're pulled from the next meet. How many have I missed? Three?

I send the same text to Rachel as well, but she doesn't reply either. They're going to be so mad.

Why did I let Madisen get to me? Actually, why was I ever friends with Madisen? Maybe if I hadn't been, she and Noah never would have dated, and none of this would have happened. Maybe it would've played out the way I dreamed it would, with Noah and I walking in hand in hand on the first day of freshman year.

My phone vibrates with a text, but it's neither Nia nor Rachel. It's Mom.

Your school called me. I'm picking you up after.

It's impossible to read between the lines if she's mad, but I don't doubt it. I've never been in detention, and Mom has never gotten a call from my school except for the one time I threw up in second grade.

But wait…pick me up? She starts work at five; she doesn't have time to do that. I start to text back that I can walk but backspace what I've written. It's too hard to convey emotion over text, and I don't want the first thing I say to be misconstrued. I want Mom to know I'm still the same good kid Katarina.

Am I though?

The Katarina I used to be never got detention, never fought in class, had friends. Oh, how things change.

I pass the time reading the rest of *The Scarlet Letter*, even though we're not set to finish the book for another month. At 4:30, Mrs. Foresta huffs and tosses down her magazine, inconvenienced by having to dismiss us. All she does is open the door, but that's enough for us. MJ is out the door in record speed, texting the whole. I gather up my things more slowly. I'm nervous to face Mom and want to put it off just a bit longer. The boy in the hoodie is still sleeping, and Mrs. Foresta has returned to her magazine, so I cross the room and tap him on the shoulder. He doesn't stir so I shake him a little. "Hey, it's time to go."

He lifts his head, and a few dark curls fall into his eyes. I don't recognize him, but he smiles at me. "You're Katarina," he says with a sleepy grin.

I sigh. "The video isn't true."

He shakes his head, pulling his backpack over his shoulders. "You're the girl that told Madisen Grace to go fuck herself! You're awesome."

"Well, that's not exactly what I said—"

"Whatever you said, it was awesome."

He holds the door open for me, and once we're both in the hallway, I pivot. "Do you have a problem with her?"

"Oh yeah," he says. "She can be a real bitch."

"Sorry…did she say something about you? What's your name again?"

"Demetrius Williams." He sticks his hand out enthusiastically. "And not about me, but my cousin. You probably know her. Nia? She's on the swim team."

"Not just on it. She's the captain."

He scoffs. "Overachiever as always." Then he winks.

"I didn't know she had a cousin at Franklin. Are you a junior?"

"Sophomore, but thank you for saying I look older."

"You could actually probably pass as a senior." He's easily a foot taller than me and only has a bit of that young, soft roundness to his face. His shoulders are already broad, and his smile is confident, like someone who has lived in his skin for decades.

"Are you flirting with me, Dobek?"

"No?"

"I'm just teasing you." He winks at me again. "Where you heading?"

I hitch my thumb over my shoulder. "Home. My mom is picking me up."

Demetrius whistles. "Oh, man, you're in trouble, aren't you?"

"I actually have no idea."

"Well, if I can give you any advice, tell your mom she looks pretty today. That usually works for me."

"Ha. I bet."

"Catch you later, Dobek."

"Nice to meet you, Demetrius. And thanks." *Thanks for not treating me like dirt on the bottom of your shoe.*

I'm halfway down the hall before I turn around, a burning thought in my head. "Hey, Demetrius!"

He turns and skips back my way. "Yes? How can I be of service?"

"What did Madisen do to Nia?"

"Oh, some bad shit. She started this rumor and then went in the girl's pool locker room and wrote in one of the stalls *Nia Williams is a*—"

"Oh," I interrupt. "I know about that."

"Pretty shitty right?"

"Awful," I agree.

He shakes his head and for once isn't smiling. "I really hate people like that."

"Yeah, me too."

"Well, if it's any consolation, Madisen seems to pick on really great people, so you must be an awesome person, Dobek."

"Thanks," I say and smile for the first time in what feels like years.

"Good luck with your mom. Don't forget to compliment her."

"Will do," I laugh.

I'm in a much better mood as I make my way towards the front entrance and pick up zone. It's amazing how a stranger can lift you up.

And how a familiar face can bring you right back down.

Football practice must have just let out because a mob of the players, all sweaty and rough housing with each other, intersect me down the hall. Noah is with them, but he's not the first to notice me.

"Oh, hey! Look Noah, it's your girlfriend!"

I don't know him by name, but I'd recognize those blonde curls and freckles anywhere—Kennedy's brother.

Before I can get my bearings, he throws his arm over my shoulders and pulls me close like we've been friends for years. "What's up, *Katarina*? How're you doing?"

"Fine…" He's all smiles but something about this feels distinctly unfriendly. I meet Noah's eyes, and he also seems uncomfortable.

"I heard you told Madisen to go fuck herself." He chuckles, and so do the other four guys, but not Noah. My gut tells me to run. His arm over my shoulders suddenly feels like a cinder block. "Bold, girl. Steal her man and then tell her to get fucked. Good thing I like bold."

I duck under his arm and quickly put distance between us. The boys laugh, and it's like a cackle of hyenas.

"I didn't steal anyone's man," I bite. "And Noah and I aren't dating." *As he made very clear, we never will.*

"Oh, come on." Kennedy's brother tries to entrap me again, but I step away fast enough this time. "Noah, you can't tell me you don't want this. A little troublemaker on your arm."

The boys are all beside themselves as if that was the greatest joke ever told. But the insinuations—that I caused this, that I'm seeking the drama—make me ball my fists.

"Go fuck yourself."

The laughter cranks up to a roar. "Damn, Kyle! She shut you *downnnn!*"

Kyle wipes a fake tear from his eye. "You're on a roll today, I see."

"Apparently there are a lot of assholes in my way today." I glance at Noah. Why isn't he saying anything? Why is he just standing there looking at his shoes with his hands in his pockets?

"Oh man, Noah," Kyle continues, "you're in for it with this one. Does she already have your balls in her bag?"

Noah's whole face, from his neck to his ears, goes scarlet. His mouth is a glued line, and he won't meet my gaze, even as I telepathically beg him to say something. Aren't these his friends, his teammates? *Tell them to stop. Tell them to stop, Noah.*

"Be good to my man, Dobek. You gotta suppress all those slutty urges—"

I just came out of detention, so I figure there's nothing left to lose. My fist is already closed and easily breaks Kyle's nose. He falls back a step, which makes me oddly proud, though my hand is stinging. I'm not going to wait around for another smartass comment, but I do glance at Noah one more time. He meets my gaze, and it feels like I'm on a ship, and he's on the dock, and we both know that this is it. I'm sailing away from Noah forever.

I don't run until I round the corner. The part of my brain that's drunk on rom coms and YA romance is listening hard for the sound of Noah's pounding footsteps as he races to catch up to me (preferably after telling his friends off). But they don't come, and I know they're not going to. I saw it all in his face; he was morphing into his junior high self and crawling back into his shell.

I should have realized it when he told me he didn't say anything to Kyle about bullying Gavin Maccabee—Noah is so terrified of being the target again that he was never going to stand up for me. Everything suddenly makes sense, and each revelation is a crushing blow. That's why Noah didn't ask Madisen to take the video down. That's why Noah wanted *me* to confront it. That's why Noah didn't comment in support. That's why Noah didn't stop his teammates.

He'd rather watch my ship sink than risk drowning to save me.

I'm gutted and completely forget that Mom was coming to pick me up until I hear two quick honks of a horn that make me jump out of my skin. Mom is parked in our used Honda by the front of the school and gives me a confused look before waving me over.

I should have been thinking about what I was going to say to her during detention because now, as I put my bags in the car and sit in the passenger seat, I'm afraid I'm going to tell her everything.

Mom looks like she had rehearsed what she was going to say to me but is holding back. I can see the gears turning, can practically taste the unasked question.

Instead, I ask, "Why aren't you wearing your scrubs?" She's dressed in clothes normally reserved for her days off, a pair of jeans so well worn they're practically silk and a Fort Clemens 5K T-shirt (Mom handed out water).

"I called in sick today," she says as she starts up the car.

Mom never calls in sick. Never, not once in my life, have I known her to do it. Knowing that she did for me makes me feel all that much worse.

It's quiet in the car as we wait at the entrance for a break in traffic to turn onto the main road. The radio is off, but I think that's purposeful. I don't want to start the conversation, so I wait for Mom to ask.

She does as soon as we turn out of the parking lot. "So, what happened?"

"What did the office tell you?"

"That you got detention for a fight in calculus."

I rest my elbow on the door and my chin on my hand and watch the neighborhood roll by. It's funny that the school calls what happened in calculus a fight when I would think a fight is more like what just happened in the hall.

"Kata?"

"We're not friends anymore." Saying it out loud, even so quietly, brings sharp tears to my eyes. I turn a little more towards the window so Mom won't see.

"You and who?" Mom asks gently. I can hear the sadness in her voice, and it makes me feel even worse. I know what she's thinking: that somehow this is her fault. That if we had more money I would fit in better; that this is just the beginning of what will happen all next year as my friends leave for school and I don't.

"Madisen." I say her name because when I try to say Noah's no sound comes out. Four years ago, when I'd lost Noah in the romantic sense, I thought it would kill me, but I never thought about how much worse it would be to lose him *completely*. And maybe I don't have to; maybe we can go on like today didn't happen and we're still friends. But what's the point of having a friend that doesn't act like one?

"What happened?"

We turn and drive alongside Juneway Beach. I see the charred remnants of a bonfire, a discarded flip flop, and the waves coming in to capture memories and take them back out to the ocean. I imagine them washing up over footprints in the sand, taking my love confession with them, and leaving the shore clear and clean. A blank slate for someone else.

"She's not the person I thought she was."

Chapter Sixteen

GOOD LUCK AT THE meet today.

It's the first thing Noah has said to me since. No apology, no explanation, just carrying on like things are normal. I guess for Noah, it is normal. I've called him my best friend for years without asking him to put in any of the work, why would it be any different now?

Except it is different. Because now I see it. I don't respond.

Glenbrook High School is a little more than an hour away, so the school rented a bus to take us to the meet. It's just barely six, and the sun hasn't come up yet, so everyone is huddled in groups in the parking lot, trying to keep warm and awake. I'm near Katie, Kennedy, and Rachel, but not quite close to enough be in their group. They're all wearing their relay shirts. I am too, but I have a sweater over it zipped up to my chin. If anyone asks (which they won't), I'll say it's because I'm freezing, but really it's because I'm not sure the girls want me wearing it.

If Kyle told Kennedy what happened in the hall, she hasn't said anything to me. But then again, it seems no one says anything to my face anymore. According to Noah, and now my firsthand experience, Kennedy's brother is a jerk, but would anyone take my side nowadays?

I feel like it's painfully obvious that I'm standing by myself, but I don't know what else to do. Sam and Isaac are with a group of the guys, and I don't want to go over there in case any of them are friends with Kyle. Nia is by the bus with the coaches running attendance and too busy to talk to me. So that leaves me looking at my phone, pretending to be busy texting someone.

"All right! Listen up!" Coach Kaitlin yells. She is her usual drill sergeant self at six in the morning on Saturday, whereas Coach Avery looks like the only thing keeping her alive is her Dunkin' Donuts cup. "Board the bus single file and check in with Nia. You'll do the same thing on the way back. If you're going to eat on the bus, be respectful and pick up after yourselves. The bus is a privilege and will be taken away if we leave it a mess. Keep the volume to minimum." She very obviously looks right at Sam and Isaac. "No shouting, and music should be kept in your headphones. We will not be making any stops until we get to the meet, so make sure you have everything you need with you."

Sam raises his hand. "What if we have to go to the bathroom?"

A few of the boys snicker.

Coach Kaitlin rolls her eyes. "You should have gone before you got here. The school is locked."

"Well, boys," Sam says low enough for the coaches not to hear, "I will be watering the plants if anyone needs me."

I file into line behind Rachel to board the bus. She doesn't say anything to me, but I don't know if that's because she's mad at me or because it's early in the morning or because she just doesn't notice me behind her.

"All right Katarina, I've got you," Nia says when I get to the front. She smiles at me. I wonder if she knows how alone I feel right now and how much just that little gesture means.

Kennedy and Katie are sitting together near the back of the bus, and Rachel is in the row across from them. She's made room next to her, so I swallow the butterflies in my stomach and prepare to find out if my team hates me. "Can I sit?"

Rachel pulls out her headphones, and relief washes over me as she quirks an eyebrow and says, "Why wouldn't you?"

I shake my head. "I don't know. I'm tired."

"You and me both. Who decided meets should start this early? Oh, my God, is that Sam over there? What is he... Oh, gross! No one look out the window."

"Your cousins are disgusting," Kennedy says. I hold my breath, but instead of telling everyone how I punched her brother in the face, she smiles and says "Morning, Kat."

"Hey, Kennedy." I guess I'm not surprised her brother didn't tell, but I am relieved. "Ready for today?"

"Always," she says with a glint in her eyes.

Sam and Isaac come barreling onto the bus together and throw their things into the seat behind us. "Oh, great," Rachel groans, "I'm going to have your bony knees jutting into my back."

"Yep!" Isaac says cheerfully.

"By the way," she says, turning around to Sam, "you're disgusting."

"What? I had to go!"

"Dis-gusting."

"What did you think I did all summer?"

"I don't want to know!"

"Would you all shut up?" Katie groans. She has a sweater balled up as a makeshift pillow resting against the window and looks worse off than Coach Avery. I'd like to be

147

sleeping too, but I'm enjoying the antics. It all feels…normal, and that's something I can't say I've felt in months.

Most people sleep on the way to the meet. A few nervous freshmen are exchanging homework and midterm study guides at the front of the bus, but the rest of us have our earbuds in and our eyes closed. I was too anxious about facing Kennedy and the girls this morning to eat a good breakfast, so I dig through my bag for my lunch and all the snacks I stuffed in there. I'm in the mood for something sweet, so I'm searching for the bag of Oreos I packed when my hand brushes something that isn't food. It's a note.

The only notes Mom and I write to each other are on those pink Post-its, so this one being on a regular piece of notebook paper confuses me. Sam, Isaac, and Rachel are all asleep, so I feel it's private enough to open it here.

I recognize Mom's handwriting immediately, but there's something different about it. It isn't rushed and slanted like it is in the bathroom as she's hurrying to write something before she leaves for work. The words here have all been thought over, have had time to be written perfectly.

Katarina,

I wish you so much luck today at your meet! I wish more than anything I could be there to see you. You've grown up so much and become such an amazing person, I regret that I haven't been there to watch you bloom.

I know there's something going on, and I understand why you haven't told me about it. I'm not always there, and that's my fault and mine alone. I want you to know though that when you need me, I will be there, no matter what. A job is a job. You are my daughter, and that is the most important thing in the world to me.

I wish I could give you more. I would give you everything in the world if I could. But I am so proud of all you have done. It's so much more than I know I ever could have. I am so very proud of you, Kata.

Love, Mom

I clutch Mom's note as if it were my only possession. It may as well be; it's now my most valuable. As carefully as I can, I fold it back up and tuck it delicately into my wallet where I know it won't get wet. It's 6:30, and Mom is probably asleep, but I text her anyway.

I saw your note. Thank you, Mom. I love you so much.

I don't expect to get a response, but before I lock my phone, I see a bubble pop up as Mom texts back. Was she waiting for me to see it this whole time?

I mean all of it, Kata. Kick butt today!

I'm left the rest of the bus ride with a big grin plastered on my face, and I don't care who sees.

• • •

Unlike Franklin High School, Glenbrook is not in a small coastal town. All of us seniors have been to Glenbrook a few times for different meets, but it's still hard not to be envious when we pass an In-N-Out Burger and a Dairy Queen within a block of the school.

The parking lot is jam-packed with yellow school buses and other teams unloading. Before the doors of our bus open, Coach Kaitlin stands at the front of the bus and begins the second of what will be about a dozen lectures—the same ones she gives whenever we travel. "Single file off the bus. Do not—let me repeat for the seniors in the back talking—" Sam and Isaac sink down in their seats "—do not go running off. Treat our host school with respect and clean up after yourselves. You'll have twenty minutes to be back on the bus after the meet ends."

"Or what?" Sam says under his breath.

"They're going to leave without us?" Isaac says sarcastically.

"You two?" Rachel says. "Probably."

We follow the coaches off the bus and through the parking lot to the main entrance of the school. It's always weird being at a different school. Their lockers are just as small, the hallways filled with names of past students' achievements, and the classrooms painted in motivational posters, but there's an otherness to it all. I could belong here, but I don't, and it feels as if the walls know it too.

Unlike Franklin, Glenbrook has two stories, and it never fails, even though we all saw the building on the outside, that the freshmen marvel at the giant staircases we pass. Sam and Isaac share my disdain and roll their eyes at a rebellious trio thinking of running up them to have a look.

Glenbrook's pool is beside their auditorium, so for meets we all pile in there. I'll never admit it, because it's Glenbrook, but I love this about their meets. For once we have real chairs to sit on, and we don't have to worry about being trampled on as we stretch by parents looking for snacks or the weekend janitors. The expansive stage, blanketed in shadow, is the perfect place to play cards (or sneak good luck kisses, judging by the way Sean steals Rachel away as soon as we've dropped our bags).

Katie, Kennedy, the boys, and I claim a row of seat in the back left, right by the exit door that opens to a hall of windows overlooking the pool. The boys will have their race first, but we've got lots of time to kill until any of us need to get ready.

"Where is Sean going to school next year?" Katie asks Sam and Isaac.

"How should we know?"

"Because you're boys," she says matter-of-factly.

"We are men actually," Isaac says.

"Why do you care where he goes?" Sam asks.

"Because Rachel is going to University of Florida."

"So?"

Katie looks at them incredulously.

"So," Kennedy says, "are they going to stay together next year?"

"Again—" Sam says.

"—how should we know?" Isaac finishes.

"Ugh! Forget you guys." Katie flops down in her folding seat and turns her back on the boys who, for their part, look incredibly confused. "What do you guys think?"

"They'll definitely stay together." Kennedy sits up a little taller and sticks her chin out. "Connor isn't going to Vanderbilt with me, but we've already mapped the drive and are planning to visit each other every other weekend."

As someone who is going to be left behind, I want to believe that distance won't matter for them: Katie and Connor or Rachel and Sean. I want to believe everyone will stay together even if they're going to different schools. However, I've seen too many sad smiles at hearing the news of my going to REJC to not know better. I don't want to be the one to say it, so I agree with Kennedy. "Yeah, they'll stay together. They love each other so much; they'll make it work."

Kennedy smiles triumphantly, but I know Katie is thinking the same as me—that they love each other as much as any other high school couple that broke up in college has.

I'm afraid this conversation is about to morph into one about our future college plans, so I excuse myself to the bathroom. Everyone knows I'm not going anywhere glamorous (or even with a pool), but I'd rather not be around to hear about how wonderful next year is going to be for them. Especially knowing that I applied to most of the schools the seniors on the team are going to--and was accepted—but can't attend when there's no scholarship for

small-town high school swimmers. Maybe if I went to
Glenbrook, I could've made it work, but universities don't
come to Franklin to recruit (even if you ask).

The women's room is empty, thankfully. Maybe it's
because we're at Glenbrook, but I keep feeling like Cayla
Ashland is going to jump out from a corner. No sooner have
I breathed my sigh of relief than I hear someone coming this
way. I dive into the nearest stall and lock the door just as they
come in.

"I really love those Berry Berry leggings!" one of the
girls says. I don't recognize the voice, so I'm guessing she's
not a Franklin swimmer.

"Thanks!" her friend says in a caramel sweet voice. "I
got a discount code online. Do you follow Madisen Grace on
Instagram?"

My heart seizes up.

"Oh, yeah!"

"Awesome! I think her coupon code is still good. It
should be one of her latest posts."

"Oh, my gosh, wait. Did you know the girl that stole
her boyfriend is a swimmer?"

Oh, shit. Oh, shit. I cover my mouth and try not to
breathe.

"No way! At Franklin?"

"Yeah, here. I'll pull up her Instagram."

Why didn't I delete that video? Why didn't I delete my
whole account?

"Oh, ewww. She's gross."

"I know, right? Look at her hair. You've got to see this
one where she's wearing a dress."

I know exactly what picture they're talking about. It's
the picture I posted from eighth grade graduation. I wore a
yellow sundress with little black daisies on it. I thought I
looked cute.

"Oh, my God. What are those? Bumble bees?"

"I know, and look at the braces."

"They're horrible! Did she have an allergic reaction to them? Is that why her cheeks are swollen?"

"She wishes. That's how they always are."

"No! Wait, go back to the recent pictures. Let me see!"

As I listen to them giggling over every picture I've ever posted, I wrap my arms around myself. I feel violated. Never did I ever think someone would go on my Instagram page just to make fun of me. Not just me now, but little me. Eighth-grade me. A little kid who thought holding hands was the pinnacle of romance and Oreos tasted better with peanut butter.

If it were anyone else in this stall, having their life judged by complete strangers, I know what they would do. Rachel would kick open the door and let the two of them be embarrassed at being caught. Nia would walk out when she was ready and go about her business as if she never heard. But I don't know what to do. I can't bear to face them, not alone in enemy territory like this. For all I know there's a gaggle of Glenbrook girls waiting to swarm the bathroom and trap me in it.

I wipe at a stubborn tear and rip off a piece of toilet paper to catch any more.

The girls stop talking. I freeze.

"Oh, my gosh, what if that's her?"

Oh, no. Oh, no. Too late, I lift my feet onto the toilet seat and try to make it look like there's no one in here. But the crack between the door and frame is as wide as a thumb and big enough for anyone to see through. I duck my head into my knees to hide my face.

Their fists hit the door like hammers on a tin roof. "Hello?" the sweet-voiced one says. Her friend giggles. "Katarina?"

The other one takes a turn. Bang! Bang! Bang! "I think that's her, Lib. Look."

I tuck my chin so deep into my chest that it's hard to breathe. I hope they both get pink eye.

"Katarina?" Bang! Bang! Bang!

This must be how the tigers feel at the zoo; caged with claws they don't know how to use, being commanded to put on a show.

My legs are cramping from squatting on top of the seat for so long, and my neck is completely stiff. Tears are free flowing now, but I bite the inside of my cheek to keep them quiet. Why did no one ever talk about what to do in this kind of situation? We used to have all kinds of bullying assemblies back in elementary school. They taught us to yell stop and get a teacher. If I say anything, I know these girls will just laugh more, and there is no getting help when your bullies are blocking your exit. Why didn't Principal Young go over what to do when you're trapped in a bathroom stall with thousands of people bullying you online daily?

They're still laughing, but it's getting more distant. I don't believe they're actually leaving until I hear the door close. They've probably got to get back for their race, and besides, they've made their point. Still, I count to one hundred in my head before I dare put my feet back on the ground. Then I check under my stall walls for any other feet anywhere in the bathroom. It's clear.

I burst out of my stall and run back to the auditorium. I'm not leaving there for the rest of the day. Half my team might be saying the same things, but at least I haven't heard them say it.

Rachel takes one look at me and kicks Isaac out of my seat in the middle. "You okay?" she asks.

"Oh…yeah." I wish I would have looked at my face in the mirror. Are my eyes red? Did I get all the tears? I keep my head bent and use my unlit phone to make sure my face is clear.

"We were just telling my idiot cousin he can't text a girl to ask her to prom."

"I still disagree with you," Isaac harrumphs. "A text can be elegant. It's modern-day poetry."

"Saying, 'Hey girl. Prom?' is not poetry!"

I'm only half tuned in to their conversation. While everyone is distracted, I open my Instagram and delete my account and then the app from my phone.

Chapter Seventeen

SCHOOLS MAY BE DIFFERENT, but pools are all the same. They all have regulation lengths, plastic lane lines that damn near take your fingers off if you hit them, and rusting starting blocks. The deck is always a roar of undiscernible noise and the bleachers a mess of sweaters, water bottles, and vending machine snack wrappers. I hate to give them credit, but Glenbrook is doing a good job of fielding who is allowed on deck so that when it's our turn, it's only the four of us behind the block.

"All right," Rachel says, visibly flustered after not being allowed on deck five events in advance, "we got this, ladies. Just like last time. Katie, how's your shoulder?"

"Oh, really bad. You know I should probably sit this one out."

"Hardy har."

"We're all good," I say, patting Rachel on the back. "We've got this."

"We'd better. I will not lose to Glenbrook."

"I second that," Kennedy says.

"Third."

"Fourth," I finish.

We give each other a good luck nod before Katie steps to the edge of the pool. I can't hear it, but I can see her take big, cheek-hollowing breaths as she wraps her hands around the edge of the block. Unfortunately, we don't have the luxury of being a pool's length away from Glenbrook this meet; their butterfly swimmer is doing the same in the lane to our left.

The buzzer goes off.

It's rare to gain a drastic lead in the first leg of a relay, so it's still anyone's game as Katie comes barreling in within fractions of a second of the other lanes. Well, not *anyone's* game. Whichever team is in the far-right lane is done for because their butterfly swimmer is only halfway through the return lap when Rachel and the other backstroke swimmers push off. My gaze flickers between Rachel and the Glenbrook swimmer. They're nearly neck and neck, but every other stroke Rachel pulls ahead.

It's barely a one second lead, but not one Kennedy is likely to give up. Her head is out of and in the water so quickly, I can tell she's hardly taking breaths.

I give Rachel my hand to help her out of the pool before I get up on the block.

"Sorry I couldn't get you more of a lead."

I shake my head. "You got me one. And Kennedy *definitely* is now."

It's true. I don't know what she did in the second I looked away, but she's a solid two strokes ahead of the Glenbrook swimmer. In swimming, that may as well be a mile.

I can sense Ashland's every move as she readies herself on the block beside me. She adjusts her goggles, and it makes me start to worry about my own. I hurriedly pull them up and then press them back around my eyes.

I almost don't hear her.

"Heard you and that guy are a thing now." She smiles at me with teeth like daggers. "That's sweet. Madisen really was out of his league. I'm glad he lowered his expectations."

I grit my teeth. "When he lowers them again, I'll be sure to give him your name."

Kennedy is on the return lap. I steal a glance at the Glenbrook swimmer; she's still behind.

Oh shit! Kennedy is already back!

I push off the block and make my dive into the water. I'm unfocused, it's sloppy, and I barely gain any distance. As I streamline under the surface, I see Ashland to my left. She's deeper in the water and further ahead than me. I kick hard, but the distance between us only grows. I'm not going to catch up without my arms, so I break the surface and start swimming like mad.

I stop looking for Ashland and focus on getting down the lap faster than I ever have. But just as I'm hitting my stride, I keep my mouth open a bit too long on a breath and gulp in a mouthful of water. It catches me by surprise, and I forget how to swallow. My brain shoots me with an injection of adrenaline. I stop panicking and choke it down. My throat burns, but I've lost momentum, and I can't worry about that now.

It feels like I'm clawing my way through mud as I try and regain our lead. My flip turn is great, and this time my streamline takes me a third of the way down the pool. I surface and put all my energy into my legs, turning them into a motor that my arms can barely keep up with. I know I'm swimming wildly, and in the back of my head I hear Coach Kaitlin lecturing us not to drop form and technique, but in the heat of a race, it feels like that's the only way I'm going to gain speed.

I know I've lost before I even make it to the end. Ashland's foot disappears from the water as she climbs out of the pool.

Time stops, and I sink twelve feet down where the water pressure is crushing. I lay on the bottom of the pool, staring up at the unfocused lights and the wavering blues of the water. Surrounded by nothing. Feeling nothing.

My fingers brush the wall.

They're going to hate me.

I pull myself out of the pool and force myself to meet my teammates' eyes. Kennedy's eyes are wide and doe-like, Katie has her arms crossed and is looking anywhere but at me, and Rachel—

"Come on," she says, as soon as I'm out of the pool. "Let's go."

I follow behind them, feeling like everyone we pass is ten feet tall and glaring down at me. Except for the Glenbrook team; I can hear them celebrating across the pool clear as day. When we're in the hall, apologies come bubbling forth.

"I'm so sorry. So, *so* sorry, guys. I don't know what happened."

"You were late on your start," Rachel says without turning around.

"I'm sorry, I—"

Katie wheels around. "You let Ashland get in your head. I heard what she said to you. She did it on purpose, and it worked."

Red hot shame rushes through me. "I'm sorry. I shouldn't have… I should've… I'm—"

"Don't worry about it," Rachel says in a tone that implies she's doing the opposite. "It's just one race."

Like a dejected sewer mouse, I trail them back to the auditorium. My arms are all goosebumps when we're met with the blasting air conditioning, but I don't put on my relay

159

shirt. I don't deserve to be on the team; I messed everything up. We would have had it if it weren't for me.

Sam and Isaac don't ask when they see us. Whatever teasing comments they might have made die on their lips at the sight of Rachel. Even staring at the back of her head, I know she's stewing in the loss, probably wondering if she, Katie, and Kennedy can compete next meet without me.

I forgo my seat in the middle of the group and abandon my bag to sit on the edge of the stage where the stairs meet the wall. No one follows me.

• • •

I would have preferred walking home to stepping last onto the bus and having everyone ignore me. I doubt the girls said anything, even though they hate me right now, but news of our loss spread fast. We won every event this meet except the girls 200 medley relay. And Glenbrook won it. If any other team had taken it from us, everyone would be a little miffed but quickly over it. But it had to be Glenbrook. It had to be Cayla Ashland.

The row at the front of the bus is reserved for the coaches and Nia. The coaches aren't on yet, but Nia is. It's cowardly, but seeing as no one else is making room for me and Sean is sitting with Rachel this time, I hope that Nia, being the captain, can't say no. "Can I sit with you?"

Nia stands, and for a second I fear she's literally going to refuse to be on the bus if she has to sit next to me. But she steps into the aisle and gestures for me to get in. "I get bus sick," she says, sitting back down. "I have to sit in the aisle seat."

"Oh. I thought you hated me too."

She rolls her eyes. "No one hates you."

"Um…" I glance over my shoulder at my team that hasn't said a word to me since our race. "I'm pretty sure they do."

"They don't *hate* you. They're just disappointed."

"Are you?"

"Well, yeah. This would have been our first undefeated meet."

"Right…" I commit myself to staring out the window the entire bus ride.

Nia places her hand on my shoulder. "It's not your fault. It happens. Quit beating yourself up."

She must not have heard. "Nia, I really appreciate it, but it *is* my fault. I—"

"Got distracted." She shrugs. "So what? Do you honestly think no one else ever has? Don't you remember when Sean missed his race entirely last year?"

"He was going to the bathroom."

She puts her hand on her hip and gives me a look. "He was making out with a St. Benedict's swimmer."

"*Really?*"

"Yes. I was there, and it was gross. But no one hated him, so why would they hate you now?"

This time I give her a look. "The video."

"Not that many people give a damn about what happens on Instagram. Do you want me to take a poll right now?" She starts to stand, but I grab her elbow and pull her back down.

"Girls from another school were talking about it, Nia. In the bathroom. I heard them."

"Who?"

"I don't know who they were."

"Okay, so why does it matter then?"

"Because…because no one wants to be talked about like that." Isn't that obvious? Shouldn't Nia of all people know that?

161

"Do you care about their opinion?"

"Well…no."

"So why are you letting what they say about you affect you?"

"Because it hurt."

Nia's eyes soften. I think she's going to hug me, but then I feel a sharp sting on my upper arm. She flicked me!

"Ow!"

"That hurt too," she says matter-of-factly. "Now are you going to go on the next six months talking about how I flicked you? Are you going to not show up to practice because I might flick you again?"

"Maybe," I say, rubbing the red spot. "That really hurt."

"Did you ever read *Green Eggs and Ham*?"

"What?"

"The book. Dr. Seuss?"

"Who didn't read it?" Did she hit her head? What does a children's book have to do with anything?

"I'm just checking. You're a weird one, Dobek. I wasn't sure if you knew Dr. Seuss."

"What does he have to do with anything?"

"Be who you are and say what you feel, because those who mind don't matter, and those who matter don't mind."

I wait for her to explain.

"Dr. Seuss said that. I think about those words a lot. In fact…" Nia moves closer and rolls up her left sleeve. On her forearm, right below her elbow crease, are the words *Mind and Matter* tattooed in loose script.

No one has ever personally shown me their tattoo before. I didn't even know anyone with a tattoo until now. I'm not sure what to say, so I say probably the lamest thing possible. "I didn't know you had a tattoo."

"I got it over the summer when I found out I was going to be captain. I knew everyone wasn't going to congratulate me."

"Why not? You deserve it."

"Some people still don't like a Black girl being on the swim team, let alone being their captain."

"That's ridiculous. What does race have to do with swimming?"

She grins. "Nothing. Exactly. Now you're getting it."

"What do you mean?"

She holds out her tattooed arm. "People that mind don't matter. And people that matter…"

"Don't mind," I fill in.

"Exactly. If someone cares about the color of my skin and thinks that means I can't be a good swimmer, they don't matter, and I don't give their racist opinion any thought. And that helps me sort out the people that do matter, like my family, the coaches, you. Race doesn't play any kind of factor to you, so you matter."

"Thanks, Nia. You didn't have to tell me all that, but I'm glad you did."

"I'm not done."

I smile sheepishly. "Sorry."

"Let's do it with your situation now. There's some stupid video floating around about you, right? Okay, so the people that care about that video?"

"Don't matter."

"And the people in your life that do matter?"

"Don't care."

"Boom. I'm proud of you." She squeezes my shoulder. "Now you just have to put it into practice."

Coach Kaitlin and Coach Avery climb onto the bus at that moment, followed by the driver. As the bus begins to rumble and gray smoke billows out of the tail pipe and around to the windows, a question pops into my head.

"Where did you get your tattoo?"

Nia doesn't blink. "My cousin did it."

"Demetrius?"

She raises an eyebrow. "No, Michael. You met Demetrius?"

"Yeah, in detention."

And then Nia chuckles so deeply, so powerfully, that the whole front of the bus stops to hear the joke. "Now there is boy who most certain doesn't mind about anything."

Chapter Eighteen

MY DREAMS ARE FILLED with Dr. Seuss rhymes pulled out of the recesses of my memory and, strangely, Minnie Mouse. They keep me rolling around all through the night, so when the sun starts creeping along my floor, I give up on sleep and go in search of coffee. There's a pink Post-it on the bathroom mirror.

> *How was the meet? Would you mind running to the store for me? Just a few things:*
> *Potatoes*
> *Apples*
> *Flour*
> *Orange juice*
> *Grandma's cereal (don't let her get the sugary one)*
> *Chocolate chips (bake cookies together this week?)*
> *Hollywood Housewives tomorrow?*

I smile despite myself. I know what Mom is doing, and I appreciate her trying to fill the void of my friends.

Noah's text is still unanswered in my phone, and last night he followed it up with a second one.

I'm sorry about what Kyle said. He's a jerk.

The apology feels overshadowed by the last part. *He's a jerk...* Are you any better, Noah, for not saying anything? And this isn't even the first time. Noah said nothing to Kyle when he went after Gavin Maccabee. Gavin might not be Noah's friend, but I'm supposed to be his best friend; don't I deserve better than that?

Grandma is already awake, folding a basket of towels in the living room. I sidle up beside her and grab one of the towels from the pile. "Good morning, Grandma."

"Good morning, *rybka.*"

"Do you want to come to the store with me?" I could go alone, but I want the company, and I also hope that if MJ is working, she won't pull something if Grandma is with me. Or if she does, Grandma can bear witness and agree that my actions were self-defense.

We don't make it out the door for another hour. I insist on enjoying a cup of coffee on the couch, and Grandma insists on finishing clipping coupons out of a mailer that came yesterday. By the time we hit the road, the sun is high in the sky, and the rest of the world is awake.

We're a week out from the beginning of the holiday season (marked every year by the erection of a sixteen-foot-tall Christmas tree in downtown Fort Clemens), but there are enough cars on the road that I lock arms with Grandma so I can pull her out of the way if need be. Although it would be pretty hard not to see her. Today she's wearing a royal blue pants suit that, with her short, round stature, makes her look a little like a blueberry. A cute, old lady blueberry.

No one's house is decorated yet, but as we get into town, all the storefronts are adorned with fall foliage garlands and there are hand-painted turkeys in the windows. A few even have Christmas lights strung up around their doors that won't be turned on until the day after Thanksgiving. Then, almost overnight, the whole downtown is transformed into the kind of candy cane lane Hallmark movies dream up. Seeing the preparations pulls at my heartstrings. Hannah's sister will be getting married in just a few weeks on New Year's Eve. I wonder how she's doing with it all, and how she's doing in general. Maybe I could reach out...

There's a chalkboard in front of Market Fresh with hand-traced turkeys in blue, pink, and purple advertising deals on all the ingredients to make stuffing. "*Lubię indyki,*" Grandma says as we enter the store.

"Yes, the turkeys are very nice." I feel robotic saying it as my focus is on seeing who is working today. There's a boy up front (the owner's son) and no sign of MJ. I breathe a sigh of relief. Without having to worry about running into her, I feel confident in giving Grandma half the list and taking our time. She goes one way, and I go the other.

After hunting down my half of the list, I wander the aisles to catch up with Grandma and make sure whatever cereal she picks out Mom would approve of. She *should* be eating the whole grain stuff, but then again, we all should be. I let her sneak the ones with dehydrated fruit and yogurt coated flakes as long as the sodium is low. That's where I thought I'd find her, hemming and hawing over which one will taste least like shredded cardboard, but the aisle is empty. I search produce and baking and even the meat section with no luck. Did she really beat me? I'm always the faster shopper.

But sure enough, as I emerge from the bread aisle, I see Grandma already at the checkout with her items on the conveyor belt. As I approach, I hear her and the cashier talking about the weather. *He speaks Polish?* I've never met anyone in Fort Clemens outside of our family that does. But...wait. It sounds wrong to my ears. That isn't Polish.

It's English.

"Very cold...yes?" Grandma says.

The cashier nods, smiling as he bags. "Yeah, I wish I wore a warmer jacket today."

I watch Grandma purse her lips; I can see her trying to filter the words for ones she knows and coming up short.

I hurry up and set my things down beside hers. I expect the cashier to start talking to me now, the way they do when they realize Grandma doesn't speak English (or doesn't 100% speak English), but this boy, with his mop of surfer blonde hair, carries on as if Grandma found the words she wanted to say. He points to the cereal she picked out and gives her a thumbs up. "Good choice. I like that one, too."

Beside me, Grandma raises her chin. It makes me realize how often she keeps her head bowed when we are out in public. "I like it too," she says.

As the cashier bags our things, I feel Grandma's hand wrap around mine. Her skin is calloused in places from years of work and smooth as silk in others from years of care. She squeezes my hand, and I squeeze hers back.

"All right, any coupons to—"

Grandma already has her Ziplock of clipped coupons out and is sliding them across the counter one by one. "These ones good," she says. Then without a hint of shame, she begins to hand him the expired ones. I brace myself. Whatever rapport she built with this boy is about to fall away.

"These ones you…" Her lips move to form the word before she breathes life into it. Practicing. The same way I've seen her as she reads her book. "…*honor?*" She looks to me to see if she's said it right, and although it sounded more like *Connor,* I squeeze her hand. It doesn't escape me that a word like "honor" would not be taught so early on in an English learner's book. Grandma learned that specific word for me. From me.

For the first time ever, I don't think Grandma cares whether or not her expired coupons are accepted. She's not even watching the cashier as he scans each one. Instead, she's looking at me. I squeeze her hand again, trying to say *I know* in that one little gesture.

I let Grandma carry the lightest of the bags and take the other two for myself. As we leave, she slides her arm back in the loop of mine.

"You're English is getting really good," I tell her in Polish.

She pats my arm with her free hand. "I'm glad. I didn't want you to be upset."

"Why would I be upset?"

"Your mom was made fun of when she was younger because I didn't speak English. I know it upset her. The last time you and I went to the grocery store, I know that girl said something that upset you. I know you were embarrassed too."

"I'm not embarrassed."

Grandma holds up her hand to say she isn't finished. "It's okay. I understand, and I want to learn English for you. I do not want you to have to fight my fights. I am a woman who came to this country with nothing, and I didn't come here to have my granddaughter be translator. I will learn, and I will be able to shop on my own. And you will not have to worry about me."

The weight of her words leaves a lump in the back of my throat. "I like shopping with you."

She shakes her head. "You are too young to be shopping with your grandmother every week. Go! Have fun. Enjoy life. I will learn English, and I will be fine."

"You don't have to," I say gently. "I'll always be here for you."

"*Rybka*, I want to do this for you."

And that's that. It's settled. Grandma holds her chin high as we walk home, pointing out things she knows the words for in English as I follow beside her, feeling swept up in the magic of the upcoming holidays. My stubborn-as-a-mule Grandma, who'd marched out of classes at the junior college, has been teaching herself English for months for me. How can that be anything other than magic?

Chapter Nineteen

I KNOW WHAT I want to say; I just don't know how to say it. Why does it feel selfish and asshole-ish to say you deserve better for yourself?

Good luck at the meet today.

I'm sorry about what Kyle said. He's a jerk.

Grandma also thought someone was being mean to me, but her response was to learn English to take the target off of me. It's different, of course, because she's my grandma. Or maybe it's not. I loved Noah like family, and I can't imagine Mom or Grandma doing nothing if someone talked to me in their presence the way Kyle did.

It's remarkable how one incident can erase six years of loving someone. Though maybe erase isn't the right word. It's more like what happened in the hall with the football team opened my eyes to really *see* Noah for who he is.

I wouldn't say he is a bad person. He's just like the rest of us, shades of grey as we navigate life and avoid the negative as much as possible. I see now, though, that there are two Noahs that split apart in seventh grade—Noah

Hamilton as he is and Noah Hamilton as I'd built him up in my head. It isn't fair of me to be disappointed that he didn't live up to be the imagined version in my head.

I always thought that when the low points of life came knocking at his door, Noah would meet them with courage and without hesitation. I also thought that when they came to my door Noah would be there with me. But he wasn't. Isn't. Getting bullied in middle school left scars that run deep— deep enough to leave me to defend myself.

It's not his fault, and it's not his responsibility to be my knight in shining armor, but it *is* what I expect of someone I love. It's what I expect of my friends. Even Hannah, whose discomfort may as well have morphed into a person for how prevalent it was in Madisen's bedroom, defended me. She told Madisen to stop recording when she accused me of sleeping with Noah, and she told Madisen it wasn't funny to lie about something like that. Maybe everything that's happened since then hasn't been perfect, but she spoke up when I needed her to. I know that if someone asked her point blank if something was going on between Noah and I, she'd stand her ground and say no. Noah didn't say anything at all.

Hunting for the right words feels like digging for landmines. I backstep and think about every way they could be interpreted before typing them. Even when I've written it all and read it through three times, feeling sure it needs to be said, I hesitate to send it. It's not just a text telling Noah I'm hurt by what he did—or rather *didn't* do; it's my goodbye letter. Goodbye to six years of pining and dreaming and believing. Goodbye to a version of my life I've held close to my chest for so long. Goodbye to Noah, my would-be-boyfriend. Goodbye to Noah, my best friend. Goodbye to Noah, the boy I unfairly made him out to be in my head.

Do you remember that letter I wrote to Anthony Schwartz in fifth grade? The one where I told him to leave you alone or else? I wrote that letter because when I asked my grandma what I should do, she told me to stand up for you. She said that's what friends do, and I still believe that. I wish you would have stood up for me on Friday. I wish you would have told Kyle none of it was true or at least told him to leave me alone. I know it would've been hard to do, but so was telling off Anthony Schwartz.

I care about you, Noah. I always have, and I probably always will. But I don't think you care about me the same way. I don't just mean romantically, I mean friend-wise too. I always considered you my best friend, but after everything that's happened with the video Madisen made, honestly, I expected more of my best friend. You haven't been there for me, Noah. You could have said or done anything to try and dispel the rumors, but you didn't. I'm not mad, and I want us to still be friends, but I also want you to treat me better.

I hit send before I change my mind and then set my phone down on the counter. I don't need to wait for a response; I just needed to get my feelings out and heard. I don't wait around by my phone either. For too long I've let everything that happened with the video consume me, and it's time to take the course of my life back into my own hands. As much as I dread it, that means getting caught back up on homework and assignments.

I sprawl on the living room floor with my books and planner. It's been months since I've written anything in it, but now I spend almost an hour noting every due date of every assignment until the end of the semester, which is in a little over a month. Then I backtrack and wrack my brain for the due dates of all the assignments I never did, and once I have them all written out, I start with the most overdue: an essay on the evolution of a character of choice from *The Scarlett Letter*. The essay was due two weeks ago, but all I have written is a shoddy introduction. I scrap that and start fresh.

Halfway through, I start to smell fresh bread baking in the oven. I have no idea what time it is, having left my phone in the kitchen, but my stomach growls like I've been starving it. Oh, shoot! I missed breakfast.

"*Babcia,* are you making bread?"

"*Tak,*" she says, and I hear her shuffling about in her house slippers. Not a minute later, she hands me a plate with two thick slices of steaming hot, homemade sourdough bread. I think I can inhale them.

"Thank you!"

"You're welcome," Grandma says, rolling her *r* just a bit. She eyes all the books and notes scattered on the floor and asks if I have exams.

"Not yet," I explain in Polish. "But I have lot of homework to do." I leave out the fact that most of it is overdue and will only be accepted for half credit. "Can you tell me when Mom is awake? I want to talk to her."

I've been thinking about this since Mom picked me up after detention, but made my decision after seeing her note this morning. I thought I was helping her by not burdening her with my problems. But all that did was make everything worse for both of us. Talking to Nia was therapeutic, and I imagine everything would have been easier to bear and less overwhelming if I'd just talked to Mom in the first place. Thinking she wouldn't worry about me if I didn't tell her what was happening obviously wasn't true. I could have saved both of us a lot of heartache if I'd just confided in her from the get-go.

Even though Mom works tonight, I know she has an hour or two when she gets ready where I can tell her all about it. I don't want to spend another minute with this secret weighing down on me.

When Mom wakes up, I've finished my two slices of bread and cut myself so many seconds that half the loaf is gone. She groggily comes into the kitchen in her sweats and 5K T-shirt, and I pounce.

"Good morning," I say, even though it's close to two in the afternoon. "I know you have work tonight and have to get ready, but can we talk? I can pack your dinner so you have time."

Despite the bags under her eyes and her overall haggard look, Mom nods vigorously. "Of course! Do you want to talk here or in my room?"

"In your room." I glance around, and although I don't see Grandma, I still make a point of whispering. "Grandma's English is getting much better, and I don't want her to hear."

Mom nods understandingly and waves me back to her room.

Her bed is already made, with her scrubs laid out on top of it, so I perch on the edge and let my legs dangle. Mom closes the door behind us. "So, Grandma's English is getting better? She's seriously learning this time, huh? That's great!"

"She told me she did it for me." As soon as the words are out of my mouth, I wish I hadn't said them. Grandma said Mom was always embarrassed that she didn't speak English, and now I've let it slip that she's willing to learn it for her granddaughter and not her own daughter. But Mom doesn't seem upset. In fact, she's beaming.

"There's nothing we wouldn't do for you, Kata."

"I know. I'm sorry for not being honest with you."

Mom takes a seat on the edge of the bed with me so we're sitting hip to hip. She brushes a lock of my hair out of my face and tucks it behind my ear. "What's going on, honey?"

I pick at my thumb and keep my eyes on my lap. It's easier to talk without seeing all the emotions pass through Mom's face. "Remember after you picked me up from school, and I told you Madisen and I weren't friends anymore?"

"Yes," she says gently.

It spills out of me like a jug of milk being tipped into the sink. I tell her everything: confessing my feelings to Noah four years ago, Noah telling Madisen, Madisen getting sponsorships on Instagram and subsequently making a video accusing me of sleeping with Noah to get more followers, the things people said in the halls, the graffiti I found in the bathroom, falling out with Hannah, the incident with the football team, Noah not saying a word to defend me, losing at the meet, falling behind in school, all of it.

Mom sits patiently listening, her hand moving from my shoulder to my lap to holding my hand and giving it a squeeze when I tell her about the text I just sent Noah.

"I don't know. Should I not have done that? I'm just so upset that he just stood there and did *nothing*. And then when we went to the store this morning, and I heard Grandma speaking English because she didn't want me to be embarrassed, it made me more upset with him. I mean, Grandma has protested learning English for what…forty or fifty years? But Noah, who's been my best friend for over a decade, can't even tell one of his teammates to shut up about me." I lift my head. "Am I right?"

Mom pats my thigh with our entwined hands. She doesn't say anything for a moment, and then suddenly her arms are around me, and I'm being pulled into her chest. A few silent tears roll down my cheeks that I wipe on her shirt before she holds me at arm's length and looks me straight in the eyes. "Listen to me, Kata. Don't *ever* feel like you can't tell me something. I'm your mom; it's my job to worry about you. You are the most important thing in my life. Know that, okay?"

I nod.

"You did everything right."

I smile a watery smile.

"I'm so sorry Madisen is treating you this way. You deserve so much better, and you don't need to keep anyone in your life that you don't want to. That goes for Hannah and Noah too. If someone isn't treating you right, you have every right to say so and stop speaking to that person. You don't have to put up with anything just because you call someone your friend."

I put my hand over hers on my shoulder. "Thanks, Mom."

She smiles, but it doesn't quite reach her eyes. "I wish you would have told me sooner. I wish I would have done something."

"Don't. What could you have done?"

"Told that want-to-be celebrity not to mess with my daughter for starters."

"No, no. Then you would have gotten arrested."

"I wouldn't have gotten arrested."

I give her a look. "You can be a crazy mama bear."

"Pshh. Besides, you don't think I'd get arrested for you?" She wiggles her eyebrows.

"I have no doubt. But I'd rather it be for something better than stupid high school drama."

"High school drama is a lot different now than when I was there," Mom sighs. "Girls would get bullied for the clothes they wore and it stayed at school. Everything's different now with the internet."

"Yeah, it really sucks."

Mom squeezes my shoulder. "Your friend Nia is right. Don't let any of these idiots bother you. They can say whatever they want to say, but it doesn't mean a thing. I can get involved if you want, though. I can come down to the school and talk with the principle."

"Thanks, but I don't know if that will help any."

"How about I harass Instagram to take the video down? I'd love to give them a piece of my mind."

I shake my head. "It won't matter. Everyone who was going to see the video has seen it already. I just have to deal with it."

"You don't have to. We can pull you out of school and enroll you somewhere else. Or I'm sure I can argue for you graduating early."

It's a tempting offer, to vanish without a trace and leave all my baggage behind. My heart flutters a bit at the thought of never going back to Franklin and never facing another person accusing me of sleeping with a taken boy.

But as appealing as that is, I don't want to throw in the towel. I've come this far, and I've endured so much. I'm not about to let these people steal the swim team and graduation from me. I won't let them push me out. "I'm all right, Mom. I want to finish out the year. This is my last year swimming too."

"What can I do to help?"

"This," I say. "Listen when I need you. Tell me I'm making the right choice."

"Always," she says. "And Kata, you *are* making the right decisions. I'm so very proud of you."

"Thanks, Mom."

She leans forward and kisses my forehead. Her lips are warm and soft and linger on my skin like a promise. "Don't be afraid to tell me things, honey. You're my number one priority."

"I know." I never had a doubt.

Chapter Twenty

BUCKLING DOWN FOR A week and finishing
assignments left and right was tremendous for my academic
career but unfortunately means I'm bored out of my skull
while waiting for our race to be up. I've spent the greater
part of the morning helping Sam and Isaac with their history
homework and then Kennedy with chemistry, but now that
they've got it figured out, I once again have nothing to do.

There was no good luck text this morning from Noah.
In four years, he's never forgotten, but on the last meet of
senior year, it's radio silence. I guess that's his answer to my
page-long text. It doesn't come as a surprise after Madisen
loudly told MJ in calculus Monday that she and Noah had
gotten back together over the weekend, but it still stings. I
truly wanted to stay friends. But in a way I understand. Being
with Madisen protects him from bullies like Kyle where being
friends with me opens him up to ridicule. I don't agree with
it, but I understand. Hopefully, one day he'll change, but I
can't hold out waiting for that.

"You have a lot of good memories with him," Mom wrote on a note Tuesday morning after I told her he hadn't responded and had gotten back together with Madisen. "Don't let this ruin them, but move forward. It's completely his loss if he doesn't want to stay friends."

I trust what she said, but it doesn't hurt any less.

Thankfully, not everyone feels the same as Noah. Monday morning, I pulled Rachel, Katie, and Kennedy aside in the locker room and apologized again for last week's loss. All three of them assured me they were over it. "Honestly," Rachel said, "if Ashland had said something to me, it would have thrown me off too."

"Or my jackass brother," Kennedy added. "Sick right hook, by the way."

Still, I've been giving practice 110 percent to prove to them I'm back in the game. I've gotten my speed back, and I'm happy to report Isaac hasn't so much as brushed my big toe. But today will be the true testament.

"You're going to do fine," Rachel says, practically reading my thoughts.

"I know. I'm just nervous. I think you're rubbing off on me."

Sam groans. "Great. Another one."

Rachel glares. "Excuse me, you would have missed your race if it wasn't for me."

"I was in the bathroom! What kind of lunatic comes barging into the men's room yelling at me to 'hurry it up'?"

"You were going to be late."

"I was on deck two races before mine!"

"Thanks to me."

"Someone should give you a Xanax."

"Someone should give you a brain."

Sensing a pending brawl, I clear my throat and stand. "Rachel, do you think we should get going now? I think it's getting close to our race."

That shuts Rachel up. She's on her feet like a soldier called to attention and rushes off to find Katie and Kennedy.

"Not you too," Sam whines.

"Hey, I was just trying to save your butt."

"Pshh. I can take her."

"I meant from Coach Kaitlin. Just because it's our school doesn't mean she wouldn't go ballistic on you for not being on your best behavior."

Sam smirks. "I think I've successfully lowered the coaches' expectations of what good behavior looks like."

"I have no doubt," I laugh. "But I also don't want to slip on your blood when Rachel rips your head off."

"Fair enough." He winks. "Well, enjoy waiting six hours in that sauna. Kick ass out there."

"Will do."

Rachel returns, having rounded up Katie and Kennedy, and the four of us push through mob on deck to stand in the vicinity of the blocks. Sam was right, we are very early, but I don't mind. This is the last meet of the season, the last meet I'll ever be a part of, and I want to soak it all in.

The sun pours in from the windows at our backs, and I stretch my arms to catch as much of it on my skin as I can. I savor the pre-race jitters, the way my muscles tighten and my toes feel light as air. Even being elbowed and jostled feels extraordinary today, like being part of something bigger than myself, like a fish in the ocean. I'll still swim after today, but it won't ever be like this again, with all of these people and all of this energy.

I meet Rachel's gaze, and I know we're thinking the same. We've swum together since the zero-depth days of songs and blowing bubbles, and now we're here on the same relay team at our very last meet of senior year. It's a clean end to our journey, like closing a book.

As the current race finishes, there's more breathing room on deck and a dip in the noise until the next event.

There's another race before us, then it's go time. Rachel is already adjusting her swim cap, and Katie is doing some last-minute arm circles. I'm running through my mental pre-race checklist when I think I hear my name floating over the crowd. At first, I think, if I really did hear my name, it has to be one of the Glenbrook girls looking to stir up trouble. I ignore it. But then I hear it again, and I *know* it's my name, shouted by a voice I recognize.

"Katarina! Katarina!"

I stand on my tiptoes but can't see much over all the heads of swimmers and coaches. "I'll be right back," I shout to Rachel and hurry towards the bleachers before she has time to respond.

There's a removable metal barricade between the bleachers and the swim deck, put in before meets to keep parents and younger siblings out of the way of the events. Almost all of the space along it is taken up by swimmers sitting on the bars or coaches leaning over to talk to parents. I squeeze behind a pot-bellied coach to nab a sliver of open space and scan the crowd for the familiar face.

I thought the sun filled me with warmth, but it's nothing compared to the sheer glow I feel seeing Mom and Grandma, wearing every article of red clothing they own, two rows back on the bleachers directly in front of me.

Grandma spots me first. She pulls on Mom's elbow, points right at me, and starts waving. I wave back and nearly fold myself in half leaning over the barricade, trying to get close enough for my voice to reach them. "Mom! *Babcia!*"

I watch the exact moment Mom goes from searching to seeing me. Her whole face relaxes, and her eyes light up. She springs out of her seat and nearly trips over a mess of spilled crayons trying to get down to me. "Are you okay?" I laugh as she hugs me from the other side of the barricade.

"Fine, fine," she brushes me off. "I'm so glad we caught you! Are you next?"

I hear the buzzer go off and glance over my shoulder at the blocks where the team is getting ready. "Yes, we're next. I have to go back in a second." Rachel is undoubtedly about to have a panic attack because of my absence.

"It's okay. We just wanted to see you and wish you good luck!"

"Don't you have work?"

"I asked my coworker to cover part of my shift. I didn't want to miss your last meet. Neither did your grandma."

There's not enough time or words to say what I'm feeling. My core feels like a mini orb of sunlight radiating out around me. I throw myself over the barricade and wrap my arms tight around Mom. "Thank you."

She pulls back and grins. "Hurry! Go get 'em! You've got this!" It's a rush of motivational phrases and everything I didn't know I needed. When I make it back behind the blocks (and apologize to Rachel), I'm more ready than I've ever felt before a race, like this is nothing more than breathing, something I do every second without even thinking about it.

The current race's swimmers climb out of the pool and Katie climbs up on the block. To our right, the Glenbrook butterfly swimmer does the same.

For a tense moment, Katie grips the block, waiting for the buzzer. No one breathes. I say a silent prayer twice. *Let me redeem myself.*

Eight swimmers launch off the blocks in perfect unison, arching through the air and cresting into the water like a synchronized dance. But as soon as they're underwater, the beauty is second place to the competition. This meet is so different than the first. We've all had a season to train and improve, and it's obvious in how small the gap is between the fastest swimmer and the slowest. This is the kind of race that comes down to a fraction of a fraction of a second.

Katie pulls ahead of the pack, but on the return lap it's too close to tell between her, the Glenbrook swimmer, and the St. Benedict's swimmer. There's no time to worry about that. Rachel is already backstroking with all her might and trying to get a lead. Even if it's just a hand's length, that could make all the difference.

Kennedy is shaking as she climbs onto the block. Her fingers vibrate like a hummingbird's wings as she adjusts the straps on her swimsuit. I step up to her side, as close as I can without us getting disqualified, and say, "You've got this, Kennedy."

She doesn't acknowledge that she heard me, but I don't expect her to. Rachel is on the return lap, and right now Kennedy is all grit and focus. Her dive is the most powerful on our team, and when she hits the water, she's a foot ahead of everyone else.

I give Rachel my hand and help her out of the water before it's my turn on the block.

My last time on the block.

I curl my toes a few times and commit to memory the way the grips feel like a ridged potato chip and the angle that once terrified me as a kid. I want to remember what it feels like to be feet above the crowd, like sticking my head up over the clouds. I don't want to forget this cocktail of peace mixed with adrenaline that makes the back of my neck tingle.

"Don't choke this time."

Her voice travels past me like leaves in the wind. Cayla Ashland will not ruin this memory for me.

I don't even glance in her direction as I crouch into position, wrapping my fingers around the edge. Kennedy's head bobs in the water, and her cheeks blow out like a bullfrog's on every breathe. I can feel how badly she wants this, how badly *we all* want this. I don't know what kind of lead I'll have, or if I'll have one at all, but I don't dare turn my head to see. All that matters is what's happening in our lane.

Kennedy touches the wall. Before she comes up for breath, I push off the block and launch myself into the air.

Time slows. I savor the burn in my lungs as I inhale deeply and hold the breath in the back of my throat. I can smell the chlorine of the water below me and feel the breeze from the vents above on my back. For just a moment, I'm flying.

The water rushes up to meet me, and I close my eyes as I break the surface headfirst. My very first swim coach's voice fills my head, telling me to imagine my legs are sewn together, to kick with complete follow through, and to make the time underwater last. When I break my streamline, I kick like my life depends on it, and when I finally come up for air, I'm a little more than halfway down the length of the pool—the furthest I've ever made it.

It's all water noise in my ears. Above the surface it's a roar and below it's a steady rhythm. My arms are two blades cutting through the water. My legs are a motor. I'm propelled forward almost faster than I can catch a breath. I see the black cross at the bottom of the pool and pull my legs into my chest for a sharp flip turn.

I spring off the wall, and for a moment I'm one long wave as I kick hard below the surface. Then I'm threading my way down the lane, straight as an arrow and just as swift. It doesn't matter that Ashland is somewhere on my left or that there's a swimmer just as hungry as me on my other side. It doesn't matter that this is my last meet, my last time competing. It's just me and my lane, and it's getting shorter and shorter.

When my fingers hit the wall, I don't pop up immediately. I stay submerged with my eyes wide open and seal this feeling in a memory too. Everything above is either miracle or misfortune, but here below the surface, it is calm and still. It's only me here, me and the water, and I'm happy. I hold onto that. It matters. It matters most of all.

No hand reaches into the water to pull me out of the pool, so I brace myself and prepare to face the loss. But when I plant a knee on deck and start to stand, I'm nearly tackled back into the water.

"We did it!"

Rachel hauls me up and wraps her arms around me like a vice. My legs are still shaky, and my heart rate is still coming down, so it's extra suffocating. "We did it! We did it! We won!"

It takes seeing our lane number on the board to believe it for myself.

Oh, my God, we did it.

My arms make a loud slap noise as I embrace Rachel equally tightly. "We did it!"

Katie hits us from the left and Kennedy from the right. We're a big ball of chlorine-soaked skin and happy tears as we bonk goggles and vibrate with excitement. Our senior year, our last meet, our last time all swimming together, and we pulled it off!

The judges and coaches near us make *move along* noises behind their lips, so we reluctantly pull away, but with the biggest grins on our faces. We're hand-in-hand, making our way through the maze on deck, when I remember Mom and Grandma.

"Guys!" They turn, and our stopping causes someone to trip into my back. He huffs as he sidesteps around us. "I'll meet you back in the hall. My mom is here." I hike my hand joined with Katie's in the direction of the bleachers.

"Go ahead!" Rachel says, still beaming like a sunburst. Something tells me there's no way they're waiting to celebrate until I'm back.

I let go of Katie's hand and duck under the metal barricade. I feel like a sheep escaped from the petting zoo the

186

way all the parents are looking at me. *You're not supposed to be on this side,* their eyes say. I don't care. I spot Mom before she sees me, and I climb, dripping on people's belongings, until she lifts her head.

This time, I'm the one that trips.

I don't lift my foot high enough to climb the bleacher between us, but just before I bang my head on the metal, two hands squeeze my shoulders and hold me still. Mom pulls me upright and crushes me to her chest.

"Mom, I'm all wet!"

"I don't care." She helps me climb the bleacher and pulls me into another hug. "You won! Your senior meet! I saw you, and you were wonderful."

"*Wspaniale!*" Grandma agrees, standing and letting me soak her clothes as well.

"You saw? I was in lane four, and I was the last swimmer. You saw me?"

Mom nods victoriously. "Yes, yes! I saw the whole thing. Kata, you were so fast! You finished so far ahead of the others."

"The girls got me a good lead."

But Mom won't hear any of it. "You were *so* fast! Oh, my gosh, I had no idea you are that good. It was so amazing to watch."

I don't worry about my wet skin and hug her tight. "I'm so glad you came. Both of you."

Mom puts her chin on top of my head, and I feel completely whole. "There's no way I would have missed this. I would've quit my job." I know, feeling her squeeze my arms and her heartbeat against mine, she means it.

"I should probably get back to the team," I say, although I'm torn between wanting to celebrate with the girls and wanting to sit here with Mom and Grandma for the rest of the meet. But Mom pushes on my back and waves me along. "Go celebrate! I'm off tomorrow, we'll celebrate then. We can go to Blue Whale."

"Definitely!"

I hug them both one more time and practically skip down the bleachers. A lot of people are packing up their things. Is the meet over already? I check the board, and we're on the second to last event, the women's 200 IM. Nia's race.

I duck back under the barrier, but instead of going back to the hallway to celebrate with the team, I lean on the metal bars and wait for Nia. She's getting up on the block now, the only one standing as she does a few last-minute stretches. Her brow is set with confidence, and she looks fierce. My heart swells with pride for her. This isn't just my last senior year meet, it's hers too, and I can feel how ready she is to dominate it.

In the echoing murmur all around, a voice from a woman behind me cuts straight through to my ears. "Where's Janey at?" Her *s*'s are long and crisp, and I picture the perfectly straight, perfectly white teeth she speaks through.

"Over there," a more honeyed voice says, "next to the Black girl."

"There's a Black girl on the team?"

"No, not on our team. Franklin's."

"You'd think they'd put her in the lane next to the lifeguard."

"Oh no, get this—she's their captain."

"No."

"I know. It was probably some diversity push going on at the school."

"How stupid. You'd think they'd give it to someone that actually deserves it."

I pivot so hard that I bang my hip into the barricade, ready to tell these girls to shut up. They don't matter, but I sure as hell mind. My eyes rake the bleachers, looking for two high school girls, but there aren't any. There's a family with twin boys running up and down the steps, a middle schooler sitting alone reading her book, and two moms in yoga pants, one with a toddler sitting on her lap. Did they really leave that quickly? Maybe I caught their conversation in passing. But just as I'm thinking this, the buzzer goes off, and the mom with the toddler says, "There goes Janey."

When Nia said she faced hate for being a Black swimmer, I imagined she was talking about our classmates or kids our age. I never thought she meant full-grown adults. But here they are, two women easily in their upper thirties, with mortgages and car payments and 401Ks to worry about, slandering a teenager they don't even know all because she's Black. My stomach churns at the blatant racism and how they both sit there without a mind.

"Hey!" I shout, hands shaking and heels unable to stay flat on the ground. My voice has all the power behind it of a store manager calling out a shoplifter, and both moms lift their heads looking confused. "Her name is Nia, not Black girl. And she's about to kick Janey's ass."

I wheel around, not leaving what I said up for debate. As I watch Nia, I try to unclench my teeth and uncurl my fingers from fists, but it's impossible. I'm fuming.

I don't know which girl is Janey, but I don't care. I want Nia to beat all of them. Not for the team and not just to shut these women up, but for herself. Comments like that would have shaken me, and I have to imagine it's only the tip of the iceberg Nia has faced, so I hope she wins this race and every one after so she remembers it's all bullshit.

"Come on, Nia!" She's already a whole arm's length ahead of the next fastest swimmer. She's only halfway through, but with every stroke she's gaining more and more distance. On her last flip turn, she's a bullet, and she makes swimming the final length look leisurely. She touches the wall with seconds to spare and comes up with an ear-to-ear grin on her face. She knows she's just absolutely crushed this race; she knows how much of a boss she is.

I leave my spot by the barricade to congratulate her and to not have to hear whatever else the women behind me have to say. The men's 200 IM is the last event, and now that they're up on the blocks, the deck behind is clear and breathable. Nia catches sight of me right away and comes over. "You did so well!" I tell her before she has a chance to say anything.

"Thanks," she says with a wide smile, despite pulling off her swim cap at the same time (a painful experience that always pulls my hair). "You did great, too. We really pulled it together for the last meet."

I bump her shoulder as we make our way back to the rest of the team. "We had a good captain kicking our butts at practice."

I see the two moms out of the corner of my eye as we pass, but I don't so much as glance in their direction. I also don't mention anything to Nia. I don't give them another second of my attention. What matters is that Nia won her race, we won ours, and our team did phenomenal. Everything else is just noise.

Chapter Twenty One

I FUMBLE WITH MY phone as I clench and unclench my toes in the sand. It's the second to last day of December, the second to last day of this year, and the winds of change are as cold as fresh snow. I bury my feet deeper in the sand for warmth and pull my hat down lower over my ears. Mom is at work, and Grandma is busy preparing a mini feast for New Year's Eve, but I snuck out for a moment of peace and reprieve from rolling dough.

I've been toying with this idea for a long time, weeks if not months. I've been waiting for the right time, and this feels like it. We're about to enter a brand-new year, and I am looking forward to a blank slate.

The dust has mostly settled on the Madisen affair. I owe that in part to the same audience that stirred up all the trouble in the first place. I've heard through the rumor mill that Madisen's Instagram page has gotten nearly one hundred thousand followers, and that has rocketed her into a whole new tier of social media influencers. Very few people (and none to my face) talk about the drama that unfolded anymore; now the gossip is all about the clothes and the shoes and the trips she's garnered from advertising.

I heard one rumor—credibility yet to be determined— that Madisen won't be going to UCLA next year but instead has taken a job with a modeling agency. It's still a bit strange to be hearing all this from outside the inner circle, but it's made it all the more clear that our friendship wasn't meant to last, video or not.

Also quelling the rumors is the fact that Noah and I haven't spoken since November. There's no anger between us (we nod to each other when we're walking home from school), but the hurt lingers. Maybe one day we'll be back to what we used to be (minus my crush), and maybe we'll make up soon, but I don't think I'm ready to just yet.

I tap my nails on my phone. *To send or not to send...* If the roles were reversed, I'm 90 percent sure I'd want to receive this text. But maybe I have a completely different idea of where we stand. I'm overthinking, but I've been overthinking for so long I can't tell what my gut response is anymore. It's all a blur of anxiety, but if I focus all my energy on quieting my thoughts then there's the tiniest tug in the direction of bravery.

I hit send and put my phone down on the sand. It's done, the ball is out of my court, and it's relieving. I take a long, deep breath, filling my lungs with the salty spray. Out on the horizon, the sky is a bloom of lavender, gold, and tangerine as the sun tucks itself under the ocean blanket. This is the most at ease I've felt in five months. Somewhere in the neighborhood, windchimes rustle and fill the air with fairy-light music. Down the beach, a table in the sand suddenly balloons in laughter.

At my feet, the sand vibrates twice. My relief is immeasurable.

Seeing Hannah's name appear on my phone again fills my heart with the same bouncy energy I had when we first met on the playground. I can't read her reply on my lock screen, but I already know we're going to be okay. It's Hannah. I should never have doubted.

All forgiven. Can I apologize in person? Do you want to get ice cream?

About the Author

Kate Greenwood is a debut author who survived middle school, high school, and college by keeping her nose in books. When she wasn't reading, she was writing (and for a brief time she was competitively swimming). Now Kate is a leisurely (i.e., slow) lap swimmer who also enjoys yoga and soaking in the sun…whenever there is any in the Midwest.

Visit Kate online at **www.kategreenwoodbooks.com** or on Instagram (@KateGreenwoodAuthor).

Acknowledgements

Thank you to everyone who helped me understand the communities represented in this book I am either no longer a part of or never have been. Thank you for helping me bring life and diversity to my novel. Thank you Bett for sharing your experiences with me and a special thank you to Alice Dearing, not only an incredible swimmer (and hopefully soon an Olympian), but a voice for diversity in a sport I hold close to my heart. Thank you, Amber, for introducing us.

For information on Alice Dearing's nonprofit, The Black Swimming Association, go to **www.thebsa.co.uk** or Instagram (@BlackSwimmingAssociation).